A Touch of His Garment

By

Ronna M. Bacon

Matthew 9

20 And suddenly, a woman who had a flow of blood for twelve years came from behind and touched the hem of His garment. 21 For she said to herself, "If only I may touch His garment, I shall be made well." **22** But Jesus turned around, and when He saw her He said, "Be of good cheer, daughter; your faith has made you well." And the woman was made well from that hour.

Table of Contents

Dear Readers

Prologue

The three children stood, in the cold rain and wind, at the graveside of their parents. Who had done such a cruel thing, to tear them apart when the children needed them so much? Who?

The oldest, a girl, gathered the two boys under her arms, cuddling them tight. An older woman stood behind them, grief bending her shoulders.

He stood and watched from the distance, a cruel smile on his face. The investigation was over. The knowledge of what his organization was up to had died with that man. He watched for a while longer, then turned and strode away, confident that the problem had been erased.

The young girl shuddered, not from cold, but from fear. Her head turned as she searched around her. She could feel the eyes that had been watching her. Would they be safe or would they too face the fate their parents had? They were too young to be on their own.

Later that night, the girl crept to the office in their home, searching for the tin box her father had told her about a week ago. She found it but couldn't open it. Her eyes darted around the room. She had to hide it, just in case. Da had said not to let anyone have it, to give it to the authorities if something happened to him. But she couldn't. It was one of her last links to him.

She found a spot, hid the box, and crept away, feeling eyes watching her even though the drapes were closed.

Please, Lord, keep us safe.

Chapter 1

Stuffing his shift paperwork into the appropriate slot, paramedic Dave Allison yawned and then headed for the locker room. He was ready to have this day end. Ten minutes later, his phone and wallet in his pockets, keys in hand, he grabbed his jacket, settled his ball cap on his head of dark brown curls, and closed and secured his locker. Waving at his work mates, he headed for the back door. He did not want to talk with his supervisor today. Ken Ellis had already approached him earlier in the day about becoming a paramedic supervisor, and Dave wasn't ready for or even sure that was a step he wanted to take.

Ken watched from the doorway as Dave slid into his car and drove away, shaking his head. He knew Dave was avoiding him after their conversation, and he really couldn't say he blamed him. It was a big decision to make, and Dave was still younger than most he would consider for such a step up. But then he knew somewhat how Dave thought. Dave wouldn't consider it a step up.

Dave pulled to a stop at the local ballpark. He was meeting friends here tonight for the game, but he really wasn't in the mood for it. He didn't know what was the matter with him. He felt restless, almost as if he was waiting for something to happen. Out of habit, he scanned the area around him. Serving four years in the armed forces had done that to him. Lord, I need to change my attitude tonight. I'm just feeling so worn out and tired in my body and heart.

Climbing the stairs, he searched the crowd, waving as he saw his friend, ETF Lieutenant Doug Foster and Doug's wife, Darcy. They had saved him a seat, thankfully, as the bleachers were filled. Not too many people missed a ballgame in his town. Then, his eyes narrowed. Darcy had turned and was talking to a younger woman sitting beside her. Dave sighed. He hoped Darcy wasn't up to her tricks again, trying to match him up with someone.

Doug greeted him, then spoke in a low voice. "Not a setup tonight, Dave. Rylee's brother is the pitcher and she needed a certain seat to get pictures for him.”

Dave nodded, greeted Darcy, then sat down on the hard wooden seat. He was bone tired and really shouldn't be here, he thought. He looked over at Darcy as she spoke.

“I'm sorry, Darcy. I didn't catch what you said.”

Her eyes studied him, and then she nodded. “I said, this is Rylee O'Shea. Her brother, Fergus, is the pitcher tonight.”

Dave turned to the woman beside him and stopped, stunned by her beauty. Dark blue eyes stood out in a fair face with a few freckles sprinkled across the nose, a contrast to the jet black wavy hair.

“Hi. Nice to meet you.” Rylee's voice was soft as she spoke, hesitant almost, with an accent he tried to place.

“Good afternoon. So, your brother's the pitcher?”

“He is, and my other brother's somewhere around. His specialty is soccer.”

“A sports family?”

Dave was trying to place where he had seen her, and he knew he had and had heard her voice.

"The boys. Not so much me. Excuse me, please." Rylee turned her attention back to the field, then looked past it. She focused her camera on the fence across from her and paled as she studied the picture. How had he found them? Her eyes flew to where her brother, Ferguson, was surrounded by his team, and then searched for Donovan.

Dave got the quick gasp she gave and turned to her. His eyes narrowing, he followed her line of sight to the fence. He studied what he could of the man, then glanced over at Doug.

"Is everything all right, Rylee?" Dave deliberately kept his voice low.

She sat back, lowering the camera, and staring at the face of the man. "I'm not sure. I thought I saw someone I wanted to avoid, but now I'm not certain it was him."

Dave pointed at the camera. "That's him?"

She looked up, studying his brown eyes with the flecks of gold in them. "I think so. I had hoped never to see him again.”

Dave studied her face, then looked across the field. The man had disappeared. “How dangerous is he to you or your brothers?”

She shrugged. “I don’t really know.” She stopped, then raised her camera again as the teams took the field, losing her train of thought.

Caught up in the action, Dave jumped at the sudden, loud whistle from near him. He turned to stare at Rylee, catching Darcy’s grin as she turned.

“She didn’t warn you, did she?”

“Warn who about what?” Rylee turned to Darcy, a puzzled look on her face.

“You didn’t warn Dave about your whistle.”

“Oh, that!” Rylee dismissed it with a wave of her hand, her eyes drifting down to the bystanders standing near the stairs. Her eyes sliding shut, she drew a deep breath. It was him, and he was here. Now, how was she to avoid him?

Dave touched her arm, and she jumped. "Your whistle?"

She turned her eyes to him, studying his face, then grinned. "Grow up on the streets, and you learn lots of useful things. The whistle is one of them."

"I've always wanted to whistle like that." Dave smiled as she shook her head at him. "Seriously, I do."

She shook her head at him again, then once more scanned the area. The man was gone, but where to?

Concerned, Dave followed her gaze, then glanced at Doug, who was staring at Rylee with a puzzled look on his face. Dave knew then that this was unusual behaviour for her. The two men exchanged glances, certain that one of them would be talking with her.

Rylee paced through the after game crowd and headed for the parking lot. She hadn't driven tonight and now wished she had. She felt herself suddenly shoved into a darkened area and up against a wall.

"Where is it?" a gruff voice demanded. "I want it. Now!"

She shook her head, her heart pounding in fear. "I don't know what you want."

She was shoved harder against the wall, arm pressed against her throat, and the voice came again, very close to her ear.

"I want your camera. Where is it?"

"I don't have it."

"I saw you with it. Where is it?"

She twisted, trying to break free, but his hold was too tight. She struggled desperately to escape. Then, she felt herself flung towards another wall, hitting it and sliding down to land in a crumpled heap. She barely heard the running feet or the thud of the man's body as he was tackled and taken down.

Dave had been on a hunt for Rylee and had heard her voice from the parking lot. Surprising the man holding her, he had taken him down, but now found himself the victim of the man's strength and anger. A blow to his jaw had him tumbling backwards and shaking his head, hearing running footsteps fading in the distance. He picked himself up, searching for Rylee. Kneeling beside

her, he reached for her arm to try and rouse
her, then pulled back as she curled into a
tight ball, her whole body shaking, her head
turned and her face hidden by the fall of her
hair.

Chapter 2

Dave turned as he heard his name called. Doug was running towards him.

"Dave! Who is it? What's going on?"

Dave shook his head and held up a hand. "It's Rylee. I found her camera and was heading to find her when I saw her being roughed up by someone."

"Rylee?" Doug bent so he could see. "Rylee?" He too reached for her with the same reaction as Dave. "This isn't right, Dave. Who'd be after her?"

"She told me tonight that she saw someone she recognized. I don't think she really wanted to meet him. She didn't say why." After searching the area, Dave turned his attention once more to Rylee. "Where's Darcy?"

"She had a meeting so headed out. I was hoping to find you to catch a ride. This is not how I thought I'd find you." Doug stood, scanning around the area. "Did you get a good look at him?"

"No, I didn't. I'm not sure Rylee did either." Dave stared at her, then up at Doug. "I'm also not sure that we'll get much of a statement from her."

Doug studied the younger woman, then Dave. Dave seemed to have picked up on something he missed.

Dave dug out his keys. "I'm parked three rows over from the entrance here, near the lights. Can you bring the car over? I want to see if I can get her attention and get her on her feet."

"Was she hurt?" Doug was concerned for Darcy's friend.

"I think so. It's more shock though, Doug. I'll know better once I get her up."

Dave watched Doug run for the parking lot, then turned once more to Rylee. He touched her hand and this time she didn't pull back from him. Reaching up, he brushed her hair back from her face, trying to assess her, but it was getting too dark. He stood, scanning the area, then nodded as Doug opened his car door. Feeling he had no choice, he gathered Rylee up in his arms and headed for the car. Rylee struggled, feeling trapped by the arms.

"It's okay, Rylee. You're safe." Dave kept his voice low and monotone. "I've got you. I won't let anyone hurt you." He deposited her on the front passenger seat, and then crouched down again. "Doug, can you get the first aid kit from the trunk? She's got some scrapes I'd like to see if I can clean."

Rylee slowly roused, feeling safer than she had in years. She blinked, hearing voices beside her.

"Rylee?" Dave's voice had her turning her head to him. "Are you okay?"

She shook her head. "No, I'm not. Don't let him near me, please." A look of distress and fear settled on her face as Dave and Doug exchanged glances.

"Don't let who near you, Rylee? Can you tell me a name?"

She turned her eyes on Dave and then to Doug, surprised to see the two. "I don't know his name. That's the thing. We never did know it. Da did but he's not alive now to tell us." Tears shimmered in her eyes, tears she refused to let fall.

Dave nodded. "Okay, then we'll see what we can do. Was it the fellow you saw earlier?"

She nodded. "It was. It seems as if he's hunted throughout Ireland and has now come to this country to try and find me. Lord, please protect us. Amen."

Dave was having trouble picking up some of her words, the stress thickening her accent. "Okay, then let's see about your face and arms. I'm a paramedic, Rylee. I'll try not to hurt you."

She nodded, still not completely over her shock. "Where are the boys? They didn't see it, did they?"

"Your brothers?" At her nod, Doug looked around at the thinning crowd. "No, it doesn't look as if they did. Do you want me to see if I can find them for you?"

"Glory be, no. They'd fuss and bother and I wouldn't have a moment's peace. Not that I will anyway when they find out." Staring at Dave, she continued, "Please don't tell them."

"It's going to be hard not to, Rylee. You have some scrapes on your face, and your arms are bruising."

Her fingers touching her face, she felt the dampness where Dave had cleaned the scrapes, then stared down at her arms. "No, I guess I can't hide this, can I? They were so young when Da and Mam died. I don't think they knew anything. Gran might but she wasn't around that much during the last year Da and Mam were alive." Dave was having trouble following the shifts in her conversation. She turned in her seat. "I need to get home. Gran will be wondering where I am." She searched around her. "Now, where did I leave my camera?"

"I have it, Rylee." Dave set it on her open hand. "Do you have a vehicle here?" When she shook her head, Dave looked up at Doug. "Then, I'll tell you what I do. I'll drop Doug off and then take you to your home. If you'll let me, that is."

Rylee studied Dave's face, then turned to study Doug. Finally, she nodded. "That's fine, Dave. I don't want to put you out."

"Not a problem, Rylee. I won't let you walk home on your own."

The man stood and watched as Dave talked with Rylee. He clenched his hands into a fist. She had seen him. He needed to get her camera as he was certain she had a picture of him. His life wouldn't be worth anything if word got out he was in the country, nor would be his associates' lives.

Dropping Doug off, Dave headed for the address Rylee gave him. Headlights in his mirror seemed to be following him. He pulled to the curb and waited, watching as the car drove slowly by.

"Dave?"   Rylee's voice held a question.

"Sorry, Rylee. After what happened, I didn't want to take a chance of leading anyone to your home, which by the way is only a couple of blocks from mine." He grinned at her. "So, you were worried for nothing.   You didn't take me out of my way."

She shook her finger at him, much as she would her brothers. "Behave yourself. If he's the man in the picture, how do I find out about him?   I know Da never said a word about what was bothering him the last few months they were alive."

"That was back in Ireland?" Dave had finally placed her accent, but not where he had seen her.

"No. In this country. But Da had been worried for years, I think." She sighed as she looked out the window. "Now, I have to watch not only for myself, but for Gran and the boys." Another short prayer for safety and wisdom escape her and Dave shot her a quick glance at that.

"You'll need to warn your brothers." She turned her blue eyes towards him, protest in her face. "He'll go after them as well. It's only fair they know. As to finding out who they are, I have a good friend's wife who can track that down for you." He pulled out a card from his pocket and wrote on the back. "Here. This is my work card, but I've put my email and cell number on the back." He handed it to her, and when she didn't take it, folded it into her hand. "You're not safe, Rylee. Let me help you find this man. Call me, promise?"

She finally nodded. "Thank you, Dave. I wasn't trying to be difficult, but where I grew up, you didn't expect this."

"It's different here, Rylee. Some people are like that, but my circle of family and friends aren't."

Dave walked her to the door of the rambling two-story house she called home. Scanning the area, he was concerned. How could he ask her about her home security? He had a friend who could help with that, but he needed her cooperation to do so.

Dave shivered as he slid back into his car. He could feel evil around him, but couldn't see anything overt. Had the man followed him after all? He prayed that he hadn't.

Chapter 3

Armed with the picture Rylee had finally forwarded to him, Dave was on a hunt for Emma Finlay, better known as Tracker. She ran an investigative firm that could find just about anything on anyone, he thought. It helped that she was married to a good friend of his, Abe Finlay, of Rebel's Elite Security. Lord, please let Emma be in today and aid her in finding this man. Rylee and her family need Your protection.

Emma looked up from her desk as Dave appeared in her office doorway and then stood to greet him. Dave smiled as he saw little three-month-old Isaac Peter asleep in his playpen near her desk, fist at his cheek, legs tucked up under his body.

"Dave, what brings you out?" Emma questioned as she hugged him.

"I need a favour. But first, how are you and your son faring these days?"

She smiled as she turned to watch her son sleep. "We're doing well, thank you. A few rough patches but it's good. Abe is over the moon with happiness, as I'm sure you know."

"I hear that. You three need to come in for a meal soon. We need to catch up."

"We'd like that.   Just let us know when."   Her keen gray eyes studied her friend.   "But that's not why you're here." She pointed at a chair as she sat back down.

"No, it's not. I'm trying to do a favour for a new friend, Rylee O'Shea. She had an incident where she was attacked at the ballgame the other night. I happened to be trying to find her to return her camera and came upon it."   He paused, still trying to puzzle it out.   "She had taken a picture of some man, and he wanted her camera."

"Is she okay?"

"She is.   A few scrapes and some bruises and I imagine some fear. The thing is that she recognized him from a distance, but doesn't know his name."

"Do you have a picture of him?"

"I can send it to your email, if you like, but this is what she sent me."   Dave handed over his phone.

Emma took it, then spun to her computer, working her magic with the keyboard. She sat back, a distressed look on her face.

"I don't like this, Dave. He is not a nice person, and he doesn't work alone. If he's in town, then his two partners are as well."

"Let me have his name and his associates' names as well. I'll stop by and see Jake Wilson or Frankie Brennan. Rylee wouldn't put in a report the other night."

"How'd you meet her?" Emma studied the face of the man sitting across from her, eyes narrowing as she caught something there. She would be having a talk with Abe, she thought. Dave was one of her favourite people and she and Abe were praying for the right lady to come along for him. Was Rylee the one?

"She was sitting with Doug and Darcey at the ballgame the other night. I was looking for her to give her the camera she had forgotten." Dave started at the floor, lost in thought, not realizing he had repeated himself. "She said something strange, though, Emma." He raised his eyes to find her watching him. "She said her father knew the man's name but never said it."

Emma sat back, turning her head slightly as the baby stirred, watching until he settled back down before she turned back to Dave. "That is interesting. I can do some research for you, if you like."

"That would be great." Dave stood, at a loss for a moment as to what he wanted to do.

Emma looked at him, and then smiled, a hint of mischief crossing her face. "How be you head over to the Irish Charm, Dave? I hear they have wonderful lunches some days."

Dave's eyes narrowed. "Now, just what are you up to, Mrs. Finlay?"

She shook her head, a smile on her face. "Not even calling me that, which I love to hear by the way, will get me to divulge any information. Call me later today, Dave."

*****

Dave stood outside the Irish Charm, not quite sure what Emma had been up to. He usually didn't indulge in fancy cakes and cookies. He sighed, knowing that she had a reason for sending him here, then pushed open the door to enter. The enticing smell of spices and freshly baked goods stopped him in his tracks. He closed his eyes and inhaled deeply, taken back to when his mother was able to bake. He looked around, noting the cream coloured tables and matching chairs, then made his way to the counter.

He turned, surprised to see an older woman standing at the counter, her eyes following him.

"What can I be getting you, young man?" The Irish lilt in her voice was strong, reminding him of Rylee.

"I was told you serve wonderful lunches. Emma Finlay sent me."

"She did, did she? Then, if you're a friend of Emma's, you're a friend of ours. What would you be having?"

Dave grinned. "I have no idea. What would you suggest?"

She tilted her head, her bright blue eyes studying him. "Wait right here, young man. I'll be back." She disappeared into the kitchen and he heard low voices.

He turned back to stare out the window. As he heard movement behind him, he once more faced the counter, stopping as he did so. Rylee stood there, a soft smile on her face, wearing a white apron with the logo of the Irish Charm on it.

"Dave! What are you doing here? I understand Emma sent you."

"She did. Now, I know where I've seen you. I couldn't figure it out the other night. I've seen you talking with my partner, Tom. He likes the scones he gets here."

"Tom and his lovely wife, Maggie. How is Maggie?"

"She's doing well, Tom said. Another two weeks on bed rest and then the doctor will consider letting her up on her feet a few hours a day. It's been a tough few months for them with her being so sick."

Rylee nodded. "I can only imagine. God has blessed them richly with their friends, now hasn't He?"

Dave stared at her. He was a believer but he had never had a friend who talked with or about God quite the way she did.

"Emma told me you serve great lunches. If I'm not intruding, would you join me for lunch?" He glimpsed the older woman watching from the doorway to the back, a thoughtful look on her face.

Rylee studied him for a minute, then turned to exchange a glance with the woman. "I can do that, Dave. What would you be liking for your lunch?"

He studied the selections, unable to make up his mind. "How about you choose what you like best? That would suit me just fine." He grinned at her as she shook her head at him.

Crumpling the papers that had contained their lunch into a ball, Dave studied Rylee. The scrapes and bruises were fading, but he could see the fear in her movements every once in a while and in the way she glanced around. He hated to be the one to talk to her, but it seemed the good Lord had placed him where he needed to.

"Rylee." Dave waited until she looked at him. "I talked to my friend, Emma."

"Emma?" She was puzzled for a moment. "Oh, you mean Emma Finlay?"

"I do. She sent me to see you today for lunch, although I don't think she was planning on us having lunch together." He grinned as she shook her head at him once again. Then sobering, he continued, "She was able to identify the man in the picture. He's not a very nice man, I would say."

"I didn't expect that he would be, now did you?"

"No, I didn't. I'm heading in to see Frankie or Jake today with what Emma has given me." He paused, his eyes searching the area around the park. He couldn't see anyone that he thought was out of place, but he could feel eyes on him. "Before you say anything, I know you didn't file a report the other night. Let me do this. If Emma is right, then they need to be aware that these guys are in town."

Rylee shook her head. "I don't want to be involved, Dave. I don't want my family involved."

"It's too late for that, Rylee. I'm sure they know who your family is. Did you remember anything else about him?"

She shook her head, then stood. "I need to get back, Dave." She was away before he could even rise to his feet.

Dave stood and watched her walk away, then once more scanned the area, his eyes narrowing as he saw a man look around and then walk after Rylee. He pitched the trash into the barrel, then walked towards the man. Hearing Dave's footsteps, the man turned and then changed his direction. Well, that was interesting, Lord. What's up with that? Then he paused. Rylee had him talking to God just like she did. He smiled at the thought. This was a lady he wanted to have as a friend.

*****

Frankie Brennan, Riverville police detective and good friends with Dave, walked towards Dave as he stood at the counter in the department.

"Dave." He reached to shake his hand. "What brings you by?" He pointed back towards where his office was.

Seated in the office, Dave hesitated, then handed over his phone, with the photo brought up. "A friend took this picture the other night at the ballgame. He also roughed her up afterwards, looking for her camera. I talked to Emma and she gave me these names." He handed over the paper Emma had written on. "She says they're not nice and into a lot of international crime."

Frankie shot a look at Dave, wondering what it was he wasn't saying. Studying the face and then the names, Frankie finally sat back in his chair. "We've had an alert to be watching for them. Something big is in the works, and we're trying to help the Irish authorities. How does your friend fit in, and who is your friend by the way?"

"Rylee O'Shea from the Irish Charm. I met her at the ballgame the other night. I'm not certain how she's involved but she told me her father knew of the man." Dave watched as Frankie stared into the distance, his face shuttered.

Frankie looked back at Dave, then sighed as he made a decision. "I don't need to tell you how dangerous this man is. If he's after Rylee, then someone needs to make sure she's okay. And it sounds as if you've made a connection with her." Frankie had already talked to Doug about the incident that night. "How close can you stay to her?"

Dave blinked, taking a moment to absorb what Frankie was asking. "I'm not sure that's even possible, Frankie."

"Make it possible, Dave. Doug approached me the day after and told me what Rylee said. If her father had dealings with them or knew them, her whole family is at risk."

"I know, Frankie, but she's not about to let anyone take over her life." Dave stood. "I just wanted to warn you about what Emma had found. Catch you later."

Frankie watched as Dave walked away, still not sure if Dave would approach Rylee or not. Then he looked back at the information he held in his hand. After a few minutes, he stood. He needed to find the police chief, Caleb Logan. He was not going to be happy, Frankie already knew that.

Chapter 4

Rylee turned as she heard her name called. Donovan and Fergus were running towards her. She waited and then turned to walk towards their home.

"How was your day, Fergus?" The three siblings were close and sharing about their day was something they had carried on from their mother.

"It was good, Rylee. Ball practice was a pain, but we're set for the next game."

"That's good. Donovan? How about you?"

Donovan had to drag his thoughts back. "It was okay, Rylee. Not much happened, thankfully." Donovan worked for a local renovator, enjoying the trade and the chance to restore old buildings. "How was your day?" He looked over her head at Fergus with a grin. They had already spoken with their grandmother and heard about her lunch date.

"Nothing really happened, boys." She was lost in thought, and her brothers exchanged another puzzled look, wondering that she didn't mention having lunch with Dave. She looked up, frowning as she saw a car parked in front of their house. "Do you know that car, either one of you?"

Both shook their head. "No, but it's a police car."

She watched as Frankie climbed out and walked towards her. "Now what?" she muttered under her breath.

"Miss O'Shea? I'm Detective Frankie Brennan. I wonder if I could speak with you for a moment."

She stared at him, then nodded. "If it's about the other night, I don't know the man. I've seen him, but never close enough to get a good look at him or even know his name."

"The other night, Rylee?" Donovan reached for her arm and turned her to him. "What happened the other night?"

"I told you when you asked about my face." She stared back at him.

Donovan nodded. "You did, but you didn't say what he wanted."

"She did, Donovan." Fergus spoke up. "He wanted her camera. And she did say he looked like the man that Da was avoiding."

Rylee stood with arms crossed, still sandwiched between her brothers, a disgruntled look on her face. "If you two boys would stop, then I can speak with the detective."

Frankie's eyes had been bouncing between the three, not quite sure what he had gotten himself into. Then, they raised and narrowed as he got a glimpse of a shadowy figure lurking near a shed at the back of their lot.

"You three stay here." His weapon was out and he headed that way. They heard him running and then a yell. He returned after a few minutes, grass stains on his shirt, having taken a tumble in trying to tackle the man.

"Are you okay?" Donovan studied him.

"I am, but whoever it was got away. I'm calling in to some backup." He stared at

Rylee. "Then, you and I are going to have a talk, Miss O'Shea."

"Not without us present." Fergus stood his ground until Frankie nodded.

Frankie slid behind the wheel of his car and just sat. He was puzzled. His eyes turned to the house he had just spent over an hour in, without gaining any new information from Rylee or her brothers. He drove away, headed for the office, and glanced at the time, groaning. He was to have been home by now. Turning around, he headed for his home. Deirdre had wanted him there tonight, but wouldn't tell him why. He never knew with her what she had planned at times.

Donovan tapped at his sister's door and then opened it.

"Are you okay, Ry?" His gaze met her.

"I don't know, Donovan." She pointed at the armchair in her room as she curled up on the end of the bed. "I really don't know. This is so unnerving."

Donovan watched as his sister bit her lip, an unusual habit for her. "Did Dave really go speak with Frankie?"

She looked up at her brother, then nodded. "He said he was. He's also talked to another friend, who identified the man from the other night and his two associates."

"Identified him? How?"

"I sent Dave the picture I took and he went to see her. It's Tracker - you've heard of her?" At his nod, she continued, "She must be good if she could identify him from that picture."

"I've heard she is." Donovan stood, then hesitated. "Listen, Rylee. You need to be very careful. Fergus and I will be with you as much as you can."

She shook her head. "No, I don't think so." She stopped speaking, staring at her brother. "I just wonder if Da had any information on him. We never did go through his things. Maybe it's time we did."

Donovan caught a glimpse of Fergus in the hallway, listening. "It's likely a good idea if we do. Not tonight, though.

Tomorrow night, both Fergus and I are busy."

Rylee nodded. "We'll figure out a time. I'll pull out the boxes we have and then see what we need to do."

*****

Pulling out the boxes in the room they had designated at their home office the next afternoon, Rylee paused. She hadn't realized they had such few, only three or four. She was certain there had been more. Shrugging, she tugged at the tape on the box, then headed for the kitchen for a knife.

Sidetracked by the doorbell, Rylee stood staring at Dave. What was he doing here, Lord? And just what are You trying to tell me, she questioned?

"Uh, Rylee. Do you always answer your door with a knife in your hands?" Dave was trying to keep a straight face, but humour shone in his eyes.

She stared at him and then at the knife. "Oh, the knife. I was wanting to open a box and had just gotten the knife when you rang the doorbell. What is it you would be wanting?" She stepped back. "Forgive my manners. Come in."

"I'm not disturbing you, am I?"

She shook her head, then motioned for him to follow. "I've pulled out Da's boxes from his office. The boys and I are planning on going through them to see what we can find out." She stopped and stared down at them. "It will be hard."

"Can I help?"

Her eyes shot to Dave at his suggestion. "Lord, you really do plan things well, don't you? Yes, you can, Dave. You don't know Da, so you may see something we don't. The boys will be home late, so they can't help."

Once more, Dave was thrown by her swift changes of conversation and enchanted with the way she spoke to God so openly and directly, just as a child would. Maybe I'm missing something there, Lord. Should I be speaking to You like that as well? He felt a sense of peace surrounding him at that question and knew the answer.

Dave handed Rylee a folder. "I'm not sure if this is something you would need to have handy."

She reached for it, stopping to stare at Dave in a distracted manner. Then, she shook her head and opened it, her hand stilling as she read the first page.

"This is it, Dave. Thank you. This is the information that Da put together. It just seems odd, though, that he would have just left it in his office." She stared across the room, Dave watching her face. Then, she leafed through the folder, searching for more information.

"Rylee, does it help?" Dave watched as she bit her lip.

"It does. Now, what do I do with it?"

"Rylee? Where are you?" Fergus' voice came from the kitchen. "Did Gran leave something for supper?"

Rylee's eyes flew to the clock. "Glory be, is it that late?" She flew from the room, and Dave could hear rattling and conversation in the kitchen.

"Fergus, have you met Dave?" Rylee's voice proceeded her re-entry to the office.

Dave stood and watched as Fergus entered behind her, a frown on his face.

"I thought we agree we'd do this on another day."

"Ferguson Daniel, that's impolite. We have a guest, who has been helping me. Behave yourself, or I'll set Gran on you."

Fergus and his sister stared at one another before Fergus sighed. "You're correct, Rylee. Sorry." He turned to Doug and held out his hand. "Hi, I'm Fergus."

"Dave Allison. Listen, I didn't mean to intrude." He stared down at the pile of papers, folders and other items they had been pulling from the boxes.

"No, it's okay." Fergus stared down at the boxes, grief briefly crossing his face. "What did you find?"

Rylee handed him the folder Dave had found as she sank back down onto the floor. "Dave found this. I don't remember anything about what there's but it's what Da found, I guess."

Fergus read through it, a thoughtful look on his face. "I guess now we know why Mam and Da were killed, don't we, Rylee?"

Tears shining in her eyes, she nodded, then glanced up at a noise from the door, rising to her feet to approach Donovan, hugging him.

Dave watched the three, then turned to Fergus. "Your parents were killed?"

He shrugged, tears near the surface. "The authorities said it was an accident, a boating accident, and they drowned. The thing is, Mam was terrified of water and would never go on a boat."

"And they were?"

Donovan spoke up. "They were on a boat. They had gone for a drive by themselves, something they often did. Rylee was watching us, and Gran was coming to stay. They never came back."

"Da was afraid that day." Rylee stared at Dave without seeing him. "I can remember the look on his face when he didn't think anyone was watching him."

She pointed at the folder. "What do we do with that?"

Dave reached for it. "I'll take it in to Frankie." As Rylee shook her head, he paused, a questioning look on his face. "You don't want me to?"

"He was here the other night and I don't think he really believed me. And that was after he chased someone from the back of the yard."

Dave stared at her, then at her brothers. "There was someone in your back yard?"

She nodded. "Frankie and the officers searched. They couldn't find anyone."

Dave stared at her again, then at her brothers. "Okay. So now what?"

Fergus stared at the open boxes and the material sitting around. "If that's all that's there, then I suggest we pack this away and take that to whoever it needs to go to."

"Wait, Fergus. We've still one box to finish. That one." Rylee pointed at the box nearest Dave. "We have time before dinner to do that. Dave, you're staying for dinner."

She sat back on the floor and pulled the box to her, oblivious to the look Dave shot her. Her brothers tried to cover their snickers, but weren't quite successful. Dave stared at them and they shrugged.

"Rylee has spoken. You're our dinner guest." Donovan smirked at him.

Chapter 5

Three weeks later, Dave reached for Rylee's hand as they walked along a path in the local park that they had become partial to. They had been spending most of their free time together.

Rylee tilted her head to study Dave's face. "You're healing, Dave, from whatever it has been that has haunted you."

He looked down at her, a slight smile on his face. She was reading him so well. "I am, and I have you to thank."

"Me?" She was genuinely surprised.

He nodded. "You've taught me to have a day-long conversation with our Father and to let Him in on every aspect of my life."

A sudden noise behind them had Dave spinning and then pulling Rylee with him as he started to run.

"Dave?" Rylee could hardly get his name out.

"We need to hide Rylee. Your attacker was behind us." Dave paused, shooting a glance behind him and then around him. "This way." He headed down a little used path, hoping it would lead to somewhere safe.

Rylee followed him down the path, her hand tight in his. Dave slid to a stop and listened, frantically glancing around. Then, a finger to his lips, he pointed to a tall shrub. He pulled Rylee behind and down the path that he had found. Dave and his friends had spent their childhood roaming this park, and the paths they used to run were coming back to him.

Finally, stopping near a tall oak tree, he wrapped an arm around Rylee and listened, their hearts pounding. He listened intently, then scanned the area, recognizing finally where they were, close to the parking lot.

"Dave?" Rylee's voice was barely above a whisper, her accent thick.

"Ssh! I'm not sure where they are, but we're close to the parking lot. Stay here for a minute." Dave walked silently the few feet to the end of the path and studied the parking lot. His car was only a few spaces away from them. He turned and beckoned her forward.

"I don't see them. We should be okay to get to my car. If I only open my door, can you climb in?"

She nodded. "Anything to get away from here." She turned as she heard sounds behind her. "I think they figured it out, Dave."

"I know they did. Come on."

Once in his car and pulling away, Dave relaxed somewhat, eyes watchful.

"Did you get a look at them, Rylee?"

She nodded. "It was him. Why is he after me, Dave? I don't know him or have anything he wants."

Dave nodded, then pulled out his phone. "Here. Call Frankie for us. Have him meet us at your place. We need to go back through those boxes of your Dad's. Were they all of them?"

Rylee finished her conversation and handed Dave his phone. "Frankie will meet us there in about an hour. As to the boxes, I was sure we had more than that, but where would they be?"

"Basement, attic, spare room?" Dave kept watching the mirrors, but didn't see anyone. He prayed the man hadn't found out where she lived.

Rylee was lost in thought. Where were those boxes? She turned to Dave. "I think there may be some boxes in the attic, but I can't say for sure. I know there's nothing in the basement, and Gran won't allow any boxes in the spare room."

"Then the attic is it. Are your brothers home today?"

She shook her head. "Not until suppertime. Gran's still at the bakery."

Dave watched the emotions flickering across her face. "Rylee, talk to me."

Her eyes trouble, she nodded. "I don't get it, Dave. Why me? What did I do to deserve this? What had Da seen?"

Dave shrugged. "That we may never know." He paused, his hesitation unusual for him. "Rylee?"

She turned to him, when he stopped speaking. "Dave?"

He shook his head. "This isn't a good time to ask this."

She tilted her head to watch him as he pulled to the curb in front of her home. "And what would you have been asking me? To go to dinner maybe?"

His eyes shot to hers and he caught the twinkle of humour in them. He shook his head. "That's exactly it. I was hoping to take you somewhere really nice, just to spend time with you."

"It doesn't matter where we go, Dave. I thought you knew that." She looked up as she saw Frankie's car pull up.

Dave slid from behind the wheel and came around to open her door. "We'll finish this later. Frankie! Glad you were able to get here."

Frankie's eyes assessed them. "Rylee's version of your adventure seemed to match your other friends. Didn't Caleb, Eddie and I tell you we didn't want any more of those types of adventures?"

Dave started to laugh, leaving Rylee to stare at the two men. He wrapped an arm around her shoulders and turned her to the house. "Our friends and their ladies have a habit of having dangerous adventures."

"And you didn't think you needed to share?"

Frankie started laughing at that. "You're having your own and dragged Dave into it. Though, it seems that's what happened with some of Abe's men."

Dave nodded. "Exactly. Now Rylee, you said you had boxes in the attic that might be your Dad's?"

She nodded and pointed up the stairs. "There a staircase at the end of the upper hall. Come on."

Thirty minutes later, Dave sank to the floor in the office. They had found more boxes Rylee remembered as belonging to her father and carried them down the stairs. She had gone to the kitchen, and the men could hear her moving around there.

"Dave?"

Dave looked over at Frankie. "What is it, Frankie?"

"What's really going on here?"

"With Rylee and her family? I'm not sure.   Her brothers don't seem to know much. Rylee remembers bits and pieces, but I think she's driven whatever she remembers deep under her grief.   She says her grandmother doesn't know much, but after today, I think we need to be speaking with her."

"I agree.   I can do that in the next couple of days. The folder Rylee gave me had some interesting data in it." He looked up as Rylee handed him a mug, one to Dave, and then left again, returning with her own cup of tea and a plate of cookies. "I must say, this is nice. Thank you, Rylee."

She shrugged.   "It's who we are, Frankie, and what we do. You come to our house, you're fed." She looked at the boxes, an unreadable look on her face. "Where do we start?"

"Why don't we each take a box?" Dave suggested gently. "If we find anything odd, we'll ask you."

She nodded, then looked towards the hallway as the front door opened. "Gran?"

"Yes, love. I see you have company."

"Just Dave and Frankie. We've found more boxes of Da's that we're going through." She rose and drew her grandmother into the room, leaving and returning with a cup of tea for her. "Gran, can you remember anything at all from the last few months Da and Mam were alive?"

Ailynne O'Shea studied her cup, then raised her eyes to her granddaughter. "I wasn't around much, but I know your Da was afraid. Not for himself, but for your Mam and you three. He had found out something he didn't want to share with me, said it was too dangerous and it was better than I didn't know." She stopped, lost in thought. Then, she stood. "He did leave a book with me that I had forgotten about until now. He said it was insurance for us if anything happened to him. Now, where did we put it?"

Ailynne rose and headed for the book shelves, her eyes running over the books. "There, love. On the top shelf. That green book." She looked around. "Oh, dear, now I need a step stool to reach it."

Dave had risen and reached for it. "This one?"

Ailynne turned and laughed. "Here, I'm worrying about getting a step stool when I have two tall men in the house. Yes, that's the one." She took it as Dave handed it to her, then resumed her seat.

She hesitated before she opened it, her head bowed and lips moving. When she raised her head, she had a look of peace on her face. "He told me if the time ever came I needed to use it, I should." She handed it to Dave. "Here. You're part of our family now."

His eyes shot to Rylee, who shook her head. "Okay. Rylee, are you sure?"

She nodded. "We are, Dave. Open it."

He still waited, his heart raised in prayer, knowing that when he opened it, there would be no going back for any of them. Frankie watched with keen eyes, knowing how his friend thought.

Chapter 6

Dave slowly opened the book, finding it a handwritten record dating back 20 years or more. He scanned through the notes, almost a diary, he thought. Then, towards the back, he found photos and receipts.

He handed the book to Frankie. "This is more your line, Frankie. Why don't you take it?"

Frankie searched the faces of the two women, then reached for the book. "Are you two prepared for what we'll find in here?"

They both nodded in agreement.

"Rylee is in danger, Detective. We need to find the men responsible and why they are after her, other than for her photos from that ballgame."

Rylee turned to her grandmother. "You knew?"

She nodded. "Donovan still can't keep a very good secret."

Rylee laughed. "He never has been able to."

Frankie had been looking at the photos and then the receipts. "Rylee, did your father ever travel to Europe after you immigrated here?"

"No. He never did. I don't think he even did before we moved here. Did he, Gran?"

She shook her head. "No, he never did. Why are you asking?"

"I have copies of travel documents, flight numbers, that kind of thing. What was your father's full name?"

"Michael Donovan O'Shea. Why?"

"Then none of these documents are his. May I take this with me?"

Ailynne nodded. "Please do. Find the ones after my Rylee and stop them. If that helps, you're welcome to it."

Frankie stood. "If you find anything more, please call me."

*****

Three days later, Dave pulled up at Rylee's home, dressed up to take out his lady, as he now thought of her. He reached for the bouquet of roses he had bought and hesitated a moment. *Lord, I am beginning to think this lady is very special. How special and where we go is in Your hands.*

Rylee's smile of welcome turned into a smile of delight as Dave handed her the flowers. She excused herself to deal with them, and Dave watched her walk away. She was dressed in a soft blue dress with low-heeled shoes. When she returned, she had a shawl in her hands. Dave reached for it and draped it over her shoulders.

"Thank you, Dave. Someone raised you right."

Dave laughed. "My mother was a stickler for proper manners. She always told me not to tease too much, but make sure my manners were there at all times."

"And do you tease?"

He grinned. "If you were to ask my cousin, Lydia, she would say yes."

"Then, I guess I'll have to have a talk with her."

Later that evening, Rylee tucked her hand into Dave's elbow as they walked along a favourite path near the river. She sensed something going on with Dave and wasn't quite sure how to approach it.

"Rylee, let's sit for a moment." Dave waited until she had sat, then he sat beside her. "I know we haven't known each other for long but would you be my girl?"

She looked up at him. "Be your girl? With what in mind?"

He smiled at her directness, what he quite expected from her. "Rylee, you are becoming very important to me. I would like to explore where we could go from here."

She searched his face, and then nodded. "We can do that, Dave. If it goes any further, you'll be needing to speak with my Gran and my brothers." She caught the smile he hadn't quite hidden. "Oh, no! You have already?" Dismay coloured her face.

He reached to touch it. "I have. Your brothers put me through about a hundred questions, though. Your Gran, she just smiled and said she knew we were meant to be."

"Gran said that?" Rylee was shocked. "No way!"

"She did. She was watching us the first time I came in and we went for lunch. I think she knew something then."

Rylee sat back, staring into the distance. "So, Dave, we're dating. Then what?"

"Then, we see where we go. And it's not just because you're in danger. You are a beautiful woman in all ways. I'm glad you're my girl." He dropped a kiss on her temple.

Her hand rose to touch the area, surprise on her face. He watched the emotions flickering across her face and nodded to himself. She was definitely the one for him.

*****

A week later, Dave turned as he heard his name called. Frankie was walking towards him.

"Heading for Mac's?" Frankie asked.

"No, not really. Were you?"

"I was. Come with me. I need to talk to you about Rylee."

"Rylee?"

Once seated in the cafe and Mac had nodded to them, Dave questioned Frankie again.

"What about Rylee?"

"We've tracked down some of those names. They're international terrorists and hitmen. What was her father into?"

Dave shrugged. "I have no idea. I don't think the family does either."

Frankie sighed. "That's about what I thought you would say. If you see her, tell her to watch herself and her family very carefully. That incident in the park? It was likely them trying to get to Rylee."

Dave nodded, then glanced at the time. "I can't stay to eat with you, Frankie. Sorry. I've had to pick up an extra shift for vacation. Catch up with me when you know more."

Frankie watched Dave walk away, concern colouring his thoughts. What had Dave walked into, Lord? Then he sighed, remembering his own adventure with his wife before they were married. How many more of their friends, Lord, would face this?

*****

Ken was on a hunt for Dave. He wanted to talk with him again about the supervisor position, but he just couldn't get Dave to talk with him about it.

"Tom, have you seen Dave?"

Tom pointed towards the parking lot. "He's already left, Ken."

"Already? He doesn't hang around long any more, does he?"

Tom started laughing, shaking his head. "You haven't heard?"

"Heard what?" Ken was truly puzzled.

"Dave has himself a lady he's dating. Sounds serious too."

"Our Dave? Dating? Ken was surprised. "What do we know about her?"

"Relax, Ken. She's a member of our church, very strong in her faith. She and her Granny run the Irish Charm. It's Rylee O'Shea."

"Rylee?   I wouldn't have thought of those two, but you're right.   They do suit one another." Ken walked away, shaking his head as Tom laughed.

*****

Rylee stood in the kitchen of her bakery, listening to the voice coming from the front.   It was him, she thought.   He'd found her.   Now, how did she get away? She spun, startled as the back door opened, and Dave appeared.   She reached for his hand and pulled him from the bakery.

"He's in the front area, Dave.   I need to get away."

Dave nodded.   "We should call Frankie."

"And why would we be doing that?"

"You're right. Come on. Do you need to let anyone know you're leaving?"

"Donovan was in the front, he's baking today, so Ellen will be fine. I'll send him a message and then he'll know."   She pocketed her phone, then turned to Dave. "How long does this go on, Dave?   How many times do I have to run?"

Dave studied her, then the area around them. "Come on, let's get out of here. We're too much in the open." Opening the car door, he tucked her inside, all the while keeping an eye out for the men. "What did you have planned for today, other than being at the bakery?"

She shrugged. "I was to be done at noon. Which reminds me, weren't you working today?"

Dave nodded. "I was, but only to 11. I was working part of a shift for a friend. So, now we have the day ahead of us. Where shall we head?"

"Taking a lot for granted, aren't you?"

Dave grinned. "I am. I was hoping to head for Oak City with you, if you were okay with that."

She studied him, then nodded. "That's fine. Any place in particular you were wanting to go there?"

He nodded again. "I have a special place in mind. And don't worry about your clothes. You look just fine to me."

She glared at him. "You should never say that to a lady when she's feeling grubby."

"Then, I'll take you by your house and you can change. How's that?"

Dave watched as she ran for the house, then scanned the area around him. He slid from the car and wandered around to their back yard, eyes watchful. He was sitting on the steps when Rylee came back out. Reaching for her hand, he stopped, just staring at her. She had changed into denim capris and a soft yellow T-shirt, and he thought how beautiful she was.

Two hours later, Dave seated her in the restaurant he had chosen, and watched as she studied the menu.

"This is too expensive, Dave."

He reached for her hands and shook his head. "Nothing is too expensive today, sweetheart."

She looked up, startled at what he had called her. Reading the look in his eyes, her face softened. "Then, what shall we order?"

He smiled. "Order what you like."

Meal finished, hand in hand they wandered through the town, ending up at a local park. Dave pointed at a bench sheltered by some bushes.

"Let's sit, Rylee."

Once seated, their conversation continued, until Dave hesitated.

"What are you thinking, Dave?" Rylee reached out her hand to touch him.

He turned, a look on his face she hadn't seen. "Rylee, I want to do everything I can to keep you safe, but I can't." He paused, upper lip curling over his teeth as he bit it. "I have fallen in love with you, Rylee." He looked up, surprised to see tears sparkling in her eyes. "Oh, there I go. I've made you cry. I'm sorry."

She shook her head. "Dave, I have seen the healing and strength you have achieved in the last few weeks since I first met you." Her fingers on her mouth, she stopped. "Is it too soon to fall in love?"

Dave stopped, eyes intent on her. "You're saying the same?"

She nodded. "I am, Dave. Gran and I had a talk the other night after you and

Frankie left. She had seen it coming." She nestled into his arms.

"Then, will you accept this?" He held up a ring with an emerald stone.

*****

Returning home later that night, Dave stopped as he approached his door. Something was off, he thought. He stepped back from the porch and walked around to the back, looking for what had alerted him. He couldn't see anything but he knew something was wrong.

Sighing, he pulled out his phone. Who did he call?

"Frankie? Dave. Did I catch you at a bad time? No, I'm not sure. Something feels off at my place and I'm not sure what." Dave's eyes searched the area again, then zeroed in on a package sitting near his garage. "I just found a package near my garage." He walked over to it. "Has my first name only. No address for me. No return address. This is bizarre."

Frankie walked towards Dave where he sat on the hood of his car. "Good thing you didn't touch it, Dave."

"That bad, huh?"

Frankie nodded. "It was a bomb, set to go off if you picked it up. What alerted you?"

Dave shrugged. "I have no idea. Just a sense of something wrong. Is this related to Rylee?"

Frankie nodded. "That's entirely possible, seeing as you two are a couple." He turned to lean against the car. "What is it with us guys? We try to help a lady out and become targets?"

Dave gave a bark of laughter. "I have no idea, Frankie, but I had been hoping it would skip Rylee and me."

Frankie looked up at the darkening sky, watching as the first stars of the night twinkling in the dark blue. "How serious is it between you two?" When Dave didn't respond, Frankie nodded. "About what I thought. Asked her yet?"

Dave started to laugh. "I'm not saying anything in case I incriminate myself. And you can tell your wife you asked and I pled silence."

Frankie broke up in laughter at that. "You know her well, don't you?"

Dave nodded, then pointed at the bomb tech heading their way. "Do you think there's one at Rylee's home or store?"

"I hope not. I sent patrol cars to make sure there isn't. What do you have for us, Bob?"

"I haven't seen this in a while. Dave, you'll recognize some of the components more than likely, from what you saw in your armed forces' day."

"So, Frankie, who is it and who's he after?"

Frankie sighed. "That's what I'll have to figure out. I'll be needing to talk with Caleb and also Eddie, I suspect." Caleb Logan was the Riverville Police Chief and a good friend of theirs and Eddie Brown was the uncle of another good friend, Abe Finlay.

Dave nodded. "And you'll need to talk to Rylee and her family. I could but it's better if it's official."

Frankie watched Dave walk away and then turned to his car, heading back home

but knowing he had just been thrown into
another investigation involving a friend.

Chapter 7

Tom reached for the cases in the back of the ambulance and handed one to Dave.

"Do you know exactly what we have here?"

Dave shook his head. "It was pretty vague, dispatch said." He squinted as he walked towards the group of young men. "Oh, no. It's Donovan."

"Rylee's brother?"

Dave nodded. "Now what or I should say who?"

Dave crouched down in front of Donovan. "What happened, Donovan?"

Donovan looked at him through blurry eyes and shrugged. "I can't remember. I can remember running towards the soccer field as I was late. Next thing I know the coach is bending over me."

Dave shared a glance with Tom, then looked back at Donovan. "Looks like you walked into a brick wall. Didn't see anyone hanging around?'

Donovan shook his head, then winced as he grabbed for the left side of it. Dave turned his head so he could assess it.

"It looks as if you've been hit with a block of wood, Donovan. We'll need to take you in so the docs can take a look at you."

"Is it really necessary?"

His coach spoke up. "It is, Donovan. I want you ready to play soccer in a couple of weeks, and you need to be fit. Humour us, okay?"

Donovan agreed, trying not to move his head. "Dave, can you call Fergus, not Rylee?"

"I can, but you know Rylee's going to find out and come."

"No. Please don't call her." Donovan knew he was begging but couldn't help himself. He knew that Rylee and their granny were off shopping today, and he wouldn't break into that.

"Okay, we can do that."

Tom and Dave exchanged a glance. Dave had told Tom what had been happening to Rylee and the bomb at his place, so both men were convinced that this had something to do with that.

Rylee stared at her brother as he stumbled into the house with Fergus' help.

"Donovan, what happened?"

He shrugged, as he sank down onto the couch. "I have no idea. I never saw anyone."

Rylee and Fergus exchanged a glance, then Fergus spoke.

"It was Dave who called me. He got the call." Once again, the two shared a look.

"Then, I guess I'll be speaking with Dave."

*****

Dave headed for his locker, ready for the day to end. Ken was waiting for him, a strange look on his face.

"Dave, I have a couple of gentlemen in the office who would like to speak with you."

"With me? What about?" Dave changed directions and headed towards Ken.

"I have no idea. They showed up, showed some government identification and asked for you.   Been up to something I should know about?"

Dave was puzzled but shook his head, grinning at Ken's comment.   "Not unless you consider getting engaged something you didn't know about."

"Rylee?"   At Dave's nod, Ken shook his hand. "Congratulations. You've found a really wonderful lady there, Dave.   Now about these guys."

Dave stopped in his tracks. "Unless it's to do with some stuff we found on Rylee's Dad." He turned to Ken. "I want you in on the meeting, no matter what they say. I'm not meeting them on my own."

"Not a problem, Dave. I didn't plan on letting them use my office without me being there."

Ken sat back down behind his desk as Dave perched on the edge of it, his eyes studying the two men in front of him. He would have known they were government officials even if they hadn't shown him their identification.

"You called for this meeting, gentleman. What do you want?" Dave took the offensive, wanting to be out of there and at Rylee's. They had planned to spend the evening with his parents.

The two men exchanged a glance, then looked back at Dave, without saying a word. Dave waited, then finally stood.

"I'm out of here, Ken. See you in three days."

"Not a problem, Dave. I suggest you gentlemen step away from the door. You had an opportunity to speak with Dave and chose not to. He's walking out of here and in fifteen minutes, you will."

"You're interfering in a government investigation." The older of the two men finally spoke.

"Don't think so. You had an opportunity to speak with Dave, and you chose not to." Ken stood. "There's the door. In future, just a word of advice, if you come here to speak with any of my people, this never happens again."

*****

Rylee studied Dave as they headed back to her home. He had been unusually quiet tonight.

"Dave, thank you for helping Donovan."

"You're welcome. He couldn't say much about what happened though."

"That's what Fergus said. Now, you'll be telling me what's going on with you, now won't you?"

Dave hesitated, then spoke. "I had two so-called government officials show up just as I finished my shift. Ken was in on the so-called meeting." Dave thought about what had not gone on. "It was so bizarre. They said they wanted to speak with me, showed me their identification and then never said a word. I left and Ken kept them there for a while after that."

"What were they wanting?"

Dave shrugged. "They didn't speak so I have no idea. I wonder if it was something to do with that paperwork we dug up." He groaned as his phone rang but ignored it.

"Aren't you going to answer that?"

He shook his head. "Not when I'm with you. You're more important than a phone call." He smiled at the pleased look that crossed her face. "You really fit in with Mom and Dad."

"You have lovely parents. Your mom is just too precious. I can see where you get your teasing from, though."

"You can?" Dave was laughing, knowing her answer.

"Your Dad." She paused as bright lights momentarily blinded them.

Dave slowed as his vehicle was boxed in. He reached for his phone, calling in their situation. "I don't like this, Rylee. Sit tight. We're not getting out." He groaned as he saw one of the men approaching him. "Well, what do you know? My mysterious government official."

"Step out of the car, Mr. Allison."

Dave cracked his window down a bit. "I don't think so. I have our patrol cars on the way. Unless you have a reason to arrest me, then move your vehicles."

"We can come up with something."

"Nothing that will stick." Dave watched as Caleb walked towards him. "There's the chief of police. Talk to him. As for us, we're out of here." Caleb nodded to him as Dave backed up and then drove over the curb and away.

"Should you have done that, Dave?" Rylee was frightened.

"Caleb will call me into his office if he needs to." He didn't think that would be happening though. He breathed a quick prayer for wisdom and protection. "On another note, did Mom ask if we had set a date? Your Gran and your brothers have."

Rylee began laughing, bringing tears to her eyes. "She did. But your dad was hilarious. He kept trying to find out if we had set a day, finally told me that we should just elope, and that your friend, Ian, would fly us to wherever we wanted to run to."

Dave gave a shout of laughter at that as he pulled up in front of her house. "Leave it to Dad. But it's a thought, you know."

"Not happening, Dave. I would like a small wedding, just our close families. It's going to be hard with Mam and Da not being there."

Dave had opened her door as she said that and reached to hug her. "I know it will be."   He stopped, staring across the street. "Go into the house, Rylee. Now!"

He waited until he was sure she was heading there, then he ran for the street. He had seen someone waiting there and wanted to find out what was going on.   As he reached the shadows, an arm slammed him against a tree, knocking the breath from him.

An arm against his throat kept him from moving. "Allison, I need your help."

Dave pulled at the arm.   "Let me breathe, man. Then we can talk."

The man eased back but stayed in the shadows, head turning to watch the area around them.

"Okay, you want my help.   Talk to me." Dave watched Rylee's house, glad she had gone in.

"You're friends with Rylee O'Shea?"

"As a matter of speaking, I am. We're engaged."

The man started, turning his gaze to Dave. "Engaged? This makes it worse."

"Makes what worse?   You've asked for my help but haven't said what or why."

The man stepped back more into the shadows as a car pulled up behind Dave.

Dave squinted. "That's a friend of mine. The police chief."

"Logan? Good. Go get him. I need to speak with him and was trying to figure out how to do that."

Dave walked towards Caleb, not sure how he was going to convince him to come with him.

Caleb turned as Dave approached.

"Dave. What did you get yourself into?"

Dave shrugged. "I have no idea. Who were those guys anyway?"

"They say they're government but there's something off about them. I asked Emma or Jace to do some research for me. Is it related to Rylee?"

Dave shook his head. "It's possible. You saw the material we gave Frankie?" Caleb nodded. "Then you know as much as we do." Dave shot a glance behind him. "Listen, Caleb, I've got myself into a situation right now. I sent Rylee into the house when I saw movement across the street. Turns out there's a fellow over there that wants my help and yours as well."

"Mine?" For a moment, surprise showed on Caleb's face. "Who is he?"

"We hadn't got that far when you showed up. He wants to talk to you."

"Then, let's go talk with him, unless you need to see Rylee first. By the way, I heard some scuttlebutt."

Dave gave a slow smile. "And that would be?"

"I hear congratulations are in order. She's a wonderful lady."

"That I know, Caleb. I'm trying hard to keep her safe, but without knowing what we're facing, it's hard."

"Then, let's go talk with your friend." He pulled out his phone and grimaced. "Your friends are causing a ruckus at the station."

"If Frankie's in, let him deal with them."

Chapter 8

Dave and Caleb headed back across the street, eyes watchful. Caleb had his hand near his weapon.

Dave stopped, eyes searching for the man who had accosted him. Movement ahead on his left had him moving forward, Caleb following.

"Here's the chief. Now talk." Dave didn't mince any words.

"Who are you and what are you doing lurking here in the dark?" Caleb tried to get a good look at the man.

The man shook his head. "I don't know where to begin. It involves Rylee's father. I knew him before he left Ireland. He recruited me to serve in a secret organization that was trying to bring to justice smugglers, terrorists, drug dealers. Her father moved here when his family was threatened."

"How'd you track down the family?" Caleb's question broke through the silence that had followed the man's statement.

"Somehow, someone saw Rylee and connected her with her father. Then they saw the boys and knew they had found the family. They're looking for evidence of what he had found. Word got back to us, and I was sent over."

"And what are they planning to do with that?"

"Blackmail for starters, I would think."

Dave spoke up. "You haven't told us your name. And without an Irish accent, I have my doubts as to whether you're who you say you are."

"I heard there were a couple of government men wanting to talk with you. Avoid them. They're not government."

A noise from the street caught their attention, and the man had faded away when they turned back. Dave and Caleb exchanged a glance, then turned to walk back to Rylee's. The vehicle that had stopped behind Caleb's brought them to a halt.

"Isn't that the car I dodged earlier?"

"It is." Caleb was getting angry, not a common event for him. "Let me call it in and I'll have them arrested for harassment for starters. That will get them away so you can get to the house. Stay here. No point in you facing them again."

Dave watched as Caleb walked towards the car, stopping as a patrol car pulled up and the officer exited. A few quiet words were exchanged, then both men headed for the car. He could hear the angry words coming from the men in the car, then watched as the doors were opened and the men removed and handcuffed. Caleb stood and watched as the patrol car moved off with the men in the back, then walked over to the tow truck he had called. When Caleb didn't move from there, Dave looked around, then headed through the yards until he could cross the street and head for another street.

He tapped at the back door to the house, and Donovan opened it, a questioning look on his face. Dave noted the lights were low just as Rylee found him and wrapped her arms around him.

"What's going on, Dave?" Fergus spoke from the kitchen doorway.

"It's those two government officials that are trying to talk to Dave. Caleb's arrested them." He could feel the tension rising in him, and fought it. He didn't need to have a flashback at this point. Lord, please help me. I can't let my friends see me when that happens.

"So, what do you do now, Dave?" Ailynne spoke from the doorway as she moved into the kitchen.

Arms tight around the woman he loved, Dave searched the faces of her brothers and then nodded. "It may help keep her safe from them if we marry soon. There's no guarantee though. Caleb doesn't think they're really government officials."

Donovan snorted. "Of course they're not. They're trying to find that information we turned in. It was all of it, wasn't it, Rylee?"

She nodded as she turned in Dave's arms. "It should have been. We've all been through the boxes and haven't found anything else." She tilted her head to Dave. "Were you serious, Dave?"

"About what?" He pulled a chair out for her, then sat beside her at the table, accepting the mug he was handed.

"About us marrying soon?"

He studied her eyes and face. "I was, but I will not rush you into anything."

Ailynne sat beside her granddaughter and reached for her hand. "It doesn't matter if Dave courts you before or after you marry, Rylee, if that's your concern. Marriage should be one long courtship." Rylee's eyes were glued to her grandmother. "That's what your grandfather and I had." She looked up at Dave. "Dave is the same, I can tell. If he feels it would keep you safe, then we are as ready as we can be."

Rylee turned to her brothers, searching their faces. When they both nodded, she turned to Dave. Silent communication went on, then they both nodded.

"We'll think about it first, Rylee. Let me talk to Caleb." Dave hesitated, then spoke again as he looked up at her brothers.

"You all need to be very careful. I was approached by a man, I'm still trying to figure that out, who said he knew your father. Caleb spoke with him briefly. That's when those guys showed up." He pulled out his phone at its insistent chime. "Caleb's put those men in jail for the night. They're not government officials after all, just like we thought."

Rylee's hand was at her mouth. "So, we could have disappeared tonight and no one would have found us?"

Dave nodded. "That's entirely possible." He looked around their kitchen. "How good's your security system?"

Donovan shrugged. "Not the best, not what we need."

"I'll have a friend come update it for you. He won't charge other than for material. His name's Joseph."

Ailynne spoke up. "One of Abe's men?"

Dave nodded. "He's upgraded mine. He's one of the best I know." He turned back to Rylee, then pulled her to her feet and led her to the living room.

"Rylee?   Talk to me?"   He was puzzled at the look on her face, not quite sure what was going on.

"It's okay, Dave. I understand." Her accent had thickened with her agitation. "I just wish…"

"You wish your Mom and Da could be here?" He reached to wipe the tears away. "Call me tomorrow."

She shook her head. "No, let's go see Greg and set up a date." She wrapped her arms around him in a tight manner. "I just wish we had met in a different way."

Dave leaned his cheek on her hair. "So do I, sweetheart."

"You'll want your sister here, Dave. Can she come back home for a bit?"

"I'll email her. She'd want me to keep you safe, even more than she'd want to be here."

"We wait, Dave. God hasn't said it's time yet."

Dave nodded, her grasp of God's timing and will always amazing him. "Just so you know, I've changed my next of kin at work and the hospital from Mom and Dad to you."

"Then I hope I never get that call, Dave." She leaned back. "You need to go. You're on duty tomorrow, aren't you?"

He nodded. He didn't want to go, but after kissing his sweetheart, he headed for the door, eyes searching the darkness. He could feel the eyes his friends spoke about watching him. He could sense evil closing in. Lord, protect my sweetheart and her family. Keep us safe.

*****

Dave yawned as he walked to his front door, key in hand. He stopped as he saw a dark figure waiting for him.

"Sorry, I didn't mean to startle you." It was the man from earlier.

"How'd you find me?"

"Wasn't too hard. Can you let me in? I promise I won't harm you."

Dave finally nodded, unlocking his door, and then locking it behind him. He studied the man standing in front of him.

"I know you."

"Thought you would. It's been a long time, Dave."

"Michael! What are you doing here, other than what you've said?"

Michael Grady was a friend of Dave's from his childhood, who had left town as soon as he turned 18. Dave had often wondered where he was.

"I've been asked to look into Rylee's family. And before you say anything, we know they are all innocent."

Dave pointed at the chairs in the living room. "I'm lost, Michael. What's going on?"

Michael sank gratefully into a chair, then watched his friend, finally nodding. "What I am about to tell you is in confidence. Rylee's father was part of an organization looking into international crime. No one knew that. Somehow he was found out, and we are tracking that leak now. He's not the first one to have been killed."

"Wow! Did you say killed? I thought it was a boating accident." Dave stopped.

"Though she did say her mother wouldn't have been on a boat."

"That's correct. Not all the evidence found on the boat has been released. Very few people know it exist." He hesitated once again. "Ben Johnson is one of those who was in the know on that."

"And he's your contact, only he retired from the force."

Michael nodded. "I've talked to him. We're in the process of setting up another contact, but we may not have time to do it before something breaks loose."

"Where do I come in?"

"Stay close to Rylee. She'll need someone to protect her."

Dave grinned. "That's not a problem. We're working on setting a wedding date right now."

Michael's face paled. "That's a definite problem. It's one thing to go after her family, another a husband." He stood and paced, lost in thought. Then, he spun. "We'll have to work with that."

"What do you mean 'we'? And how do we work with that?" Dave was on his feet, a look on his face that Michael recognized from their youth.

Michael held up a hand. "Listen, Dave. You need to work with me. We'll do our best to keep all of you safe, but our first priority is Rylee. She may know something that she's forgotten or doesn't think important. They'll go after you to get to her."

Dave shook his head, then looked at the clock. "I'm sorry, Michael. This is all too much to take in. Listen, you can use the spare room if you like."

Michael shook his head. "Can I get out through your back yard?"

Dave nodded and watched as Michael slipped away. Lord, what did I walk into? I feel like I'm back on the war front again.

Chapter 9

Throwing the towel he was folding on the dryer, Dave headed for the front door about a week later. He wasn't expecting anyone that he knew of. He pulled the door open and stopped, reaching finally for the young woman standing there.

"Liana, when did you get home? And how?"

"Early this morning, and by plane of course. Dad picked me up. We didn't say anything to you in case I couldn't swing it." She stepped back from her brother, her hands on his upper arms and saw the changes that had come to his face. "I heard my brother was getting married, and I had promised to be there when and if he ever did."

Dave gave a shout of laughter, then hugged his sister again. "We did promise that, didn't we, sis? Come on in to the kitchen. I have some of that tea you used to like."

"Sounds good." She looked around Dave's home as they moved through it. "I like the changes you've made."

Dave smiled. "That would be Rylee. She's already putting her stamp on our home."

Liana turned back to her brother and took the mug he offered her, wandering around the kitchen. "She's good for you, Dave. You're more relaxed."

"She's done more for me than anyone in the health care field has done. She's taught me how to talk to God in a whole new way."

Liana smiled. "She has? Oh, I like to hear that. How?"

"She talks to God as if He's right beside her all the time. When I realized how true that was, that's what I started to do."

Liana smiled. "That's what I told you years ago, when you came back home. Took you a while to realize it. Now, about your wedding. Anything I can do to help?"

"I'll take you over this afternoon and you can talk to Rylee and her grandmother. Mom's been involved."

Liana nodded, then turned back to her brother. Both had the brown curly hair and curious coloured brown eyes. "She's your heart, isn't she, Dave? She's the one you told me about when we were teenagers."

"She is, Liana. People have wondered why I never dated, but it wasn't fair to the ladies."

"I'm the same, Dave. Until I find that man God wants, I won't date." She hesitated, then continued. "I've often wondered about all those friends we had over the years, what happened to them. You had a friend that left so suddenly when he turned 18."

Dave froze, not wanting to hear the name, but he knew. "Michael?"

"Michael. Do you ever hear from him?"

Dave had turned away to school his face. How could he say no when he had just spoken with him again that morning? Was he the one Liana had been interested in? If he was, she had kept her secret well hidden.

"Not until recently. I spoke with him the other day but he didn't say much of where he's been."

She nodded, a sadness crossing her face. "He was always fighting something within himself. I could never figure it out. God's brought him to mind a lot lately."

"And Dad taught us that if we thought of someone, God was having us pray for them, even at the mention of their name."

She nodded, a glimmer of tears in her eyes. "He didn't have a good home life, not like we did. I think that's why he spent so much time with you."

Dave nodded as he glanced at the clock. "Come on. Rylee's likely home by now. I'll take you to meet her." He watched his sister. "We need to talk, Liana. There's more to your coming home than what you've said."

She looked up at him, startled, then nodded. "There is, Dave. I'll not be going back. They're pulling the mission team. It's gotten too dangerous there."

He reached to hug his sister, then arm around her, led her to his car and tucked her inside. Lord, how do I help my sister, help mend her breaking heart? My plate feels so full right now. I need Your strength and wisdom.

Rylee turned as she heard her name called and her face lit up. Dave was walking towards her and enveloped her in a hug, dropping a kiss on her upraised mouth.

"You're here early, Dave. I was just getting home."

"I know. I was hoping you would be." He leaned back to look down at her. "I have someone you need to meet."

"You do, do you? And who would that be?"

He turned her to face Liana. "This is my sister, Liana, Rylee. She's back home now."

Rylee studied the younger woman in front of her, knowing that there was not that much of an age difference between the siblings. At the look of uncertainty on Liana's face, Rylee reached for her, drawing her into a hug. "I'm so glad you're here. I have wanted to meet the sister of the man I love."

Liana's eyes shot to Dave. Emotion had thickened Rylee's accent and she was having trouble following her words.

Dave laughed at his sister. "She's glad you're here, Liana. Her accent thickens at times."

Rylee reached back to give Dave a playful smack on the arm, then shivered. "Can we go inside now?" She exchanged a look with Dave.

"I think that's likely the best. When are Gran and the boys due home?"

Dave waited until the two women had disappeared, then turned in a slow circle to scan the area. He knew someone was out there, but was it friend or foe?

*****

Late that night, Dave sank into a chair on his back deck. He hadn't put on any outdoor lights and the only light was what came through from the front of the house. He was tired but content. His whole family was together in town once more, and his sister and his fiancee had gotten along. Hearing a slight noise, he turned his head as a dark form approached.

"Michael. There's a cup of coffee sitting on the table near that chair for you. I figured you'd be around tonight."

"Thanks, Dave. It's appreciated. Having to stay in the shadows is not all it's cracked up to be." He leant back in the chair, his face turned up to the sky.

"Where do we stand, Michael?"

Michael shook his head. "Not where we should, Dave, not where we should. We're missing a piece of information that would tie it all together. I still have the feeling it's in Rylee's possession, but she doesn't know that."

"That's what I thought." Dave paused, then continued, his eyes on the man seated near him. "Liana arrived back in town today. She was asking about you."

Michael stiffened, then forced himself to relax. "Is she? Where has she been?"

"She was overseas on a mission, but they've brought everyone back." Dave set his coffee cup down. "Back to Rylee. What kind of information are you looking for? And can you come out of hiding to help look for it? This is your hometown. No one would think it odd if you came around again. And seeing as we were good friends, who would think it strange if you came to see me?"

Michael stared at Dave, realizing Dave had just solved his problem. "You're right, Dave.   There's no reason for me to be lurking around in the dark. I don't have a home here anymore though, and I hate motels."

"You remember Abe Finlay?"   At Michael's nod, Dave continued, "Talk to Abe. He has some cottages he might rent you. If not, talk to Ben and Marg Johnson. If I remember rightly, they were good friends with your parents."

Michael shook his head. "Here you are, solving everything for me. Now, if you could only solve the case."

"That I'm working on."

Chapter 10

It started off quiet, but Dave's day quickly headed into an extremely busy, hectic day. He turned to Tom as they were heading for their latest run, likely the last one for the day.

"What's going on today, Tom? It hasn't been this busy in weeks."

"I know. It's crazy." Tom slowed the heavy ambulance and stopped behind a car. "This looks like where we were to called to."

Dave jumped down, calling behind him. "I'll check it out if you get the equipment."

Dave hesitated as he walked towards the small red car, searching the area around him. Something felt off about the call, but he shrugged. Someone needed him and it was his duty to respond.

A sudden loud yell from Tom and the loud revving of a motor caught his attention as he neared the back bumper of the car. He turned, seeing a large truck speeding his way, heading for the car. He jumped for the embankment, but not in time to prevent his lower body being hit in passing as the car was shoved towards him. He tumbled down the embankment and lay still.

Tom dropped his equipment boxes, grabbing for his radio.

"Dispatch, we need patrol. Dave's just been hit." He ran for the car first and stopped, not sure what he was seeing. It was a dummy sitting in the front seat. He then spun, sliding down the embankment to his partner and friend, reaching out to touch his back.

"Dave, can you hear me? Dave?" He could hear the distant roar of oncoming sirens, but disregarded them as he assessed Dave.

Ken dropped down beside him. He had been out on patrol when the call came in.

"How is he?"

"Not sure yet, Ken. He took a pretty good hit from that car."

Ken stood as he nodded and assessed the scene. "I have Paul and Carol on their way. They'll take over for you." At Tom's protest, he held up his hand.   "I know. Dave's your partner, but I need two of you with him.   Besides, you're a witness and they'll be wanting to talk with you."   He stared back down at Dave. "Do you have Rylee's number?"   When Tom shook his head, he spoke. "No, I'll go get her."

Tom stood back as he watched the new team of paramedics take over, then turned as he felt his arm touched.   Ken stood there again.

"You need to come give your statement, Tom. I've put your gear back in your vehicle."

Tom nodded, following Ken to the waiting officer.

As he was giving his statement, he stopped, turning to face the vehicle.   The truck had disappeared, of course, he thought. Then he turned to the officer.

"It was deliberate. It was as if he was waiting for Dave to walk towards the vehicle. I didn't see or hear anything until Dave was near the car, and then the truck was there."

The officer looked up, frowning. "Dave doesn't have any enemies. At least, none that we know of."

Tom vigorously shook his head. "He doesn't. Never has. He gathers friends and acquaintances, not enemies."

Rylee had looked up from the cookies she was icing when her Gran appeared with Ken. Dropping everything, she had gone with Ken and now sat in the Emergency Department waiting room, almost frozen in place. Ken paced the area, every once in a while throwing her a glance, then speaking with various of the paramedics who dropped in for word.

Feeling someone touch her arm, Rylee looked up. Dave's mother sat beside her, then drew her into a hug.

"Any word yet, Rylee?"

Rylee shook her head. "Not yet, other than a nurse was out to tell me they were assessing Dave and that they were sending him for imaging, I think they said." She looked past Miriam to Dave's father, Daniel. "Can I get you two anything?" She shook her head. "No, that's not what I want to say." Tears were making her accent thicker than normal.

Daniel reached for her hand. "Not a thing, my dear. We're here to be with you and Dave. Liana was out somewhere, trying to restore her link to this country."

Rylee nodded before her eyes once more sought the entrance to where Dave lay. She had been there for over an hour already, and her fear was growing with each moment. She started as she felt someone's arm come around her.

"He's in God's hands, Rylee." Miriam's soft voice reached her, and she sat back. "We need to remember that God is in control of everything."

"And I've been forgetting just that." Rylee stared across the room, tears close to the surface. "Lord, forgive me. It's one of those times You need to hit me over the head. You have Your hand on him."

Miriam and Daniel exchanged glances, slightly astonished at the way Rylee had responded. Dave had warned them, but this was the first time they had experienced a Rylee prayer.

Daniel looked up as he felt someone near him and stood. His niece, Lydia and her husband, Ian, stood there, puzzlement on their faces. Daniel went to speak just as the nurse came for Rylee and she headed back with her.

"Uncle Daniel, what's going on?"

"It's Dave. He's been hurt." Daniel missed the look on Lydia's face. Ian didn't and knew he would be speaking with his wife about her attitude.

"Why are you out here and not in there?"

"It's not our place now, Lydia." Daniel turned as Miriam stood. The nurse was heading their way.

"What do you mean, it's not your place? He's your son, isn't he?"

Daniel finally caught her tone of voice and turned stern eyes on her, catching the look on Ian's face as he did so. It was Ian's place to deal with his wife, but Daniel had to speak up.

"No, it's not, Lydia. We're no longer his first contact in medical emergencies."

He followed his wife towards the door to the ward.

Lydia stood, flabbergasted, then spun to her husband. "What did he mean, Ian?"

Ian tugged her with him outside. "Your attitude isn't right, Lydia. It's not your place to question." She stared at him. "No, it's not your place. Sometimes you speak up when you shouldn't and this is one of them. Haven't you been listening to the scuttlebutt going the rounds?"

She shook her head. "About Dave?"

"Yes, about Dave. Your uncle told me on Sunday that Dave and Rylee are engaged and are planning their wedding."

Lydia stared at him, wondering how she had missed that. "Oh, Ian. I need to apologize to them."

Ian stopped her before she could move. "Later, sweetheart. Right now, you need time with God. Let's go."

*****

Rylee stood facing the physician, John Thompson. She had seen him at church, but didn't know him.

"Rylee, you know Dave has you as his next of kin?" When she nodded, John continued, "Right now, we'll be taking him for some X-Rays. He's pretty sore along his left side and we want to ensure there is nothing fractured."

She nodded. "Can I see him?" she asked, her voice barely above a whisper. She felt Miriam's arm around her shoulders.

John agreed. "Just for a few minutes. Miriam, Daniel. Let her go in and then I'll come get you in a couple of minutes."

Dave stirred, pain wracking his body. Flashes of memory took him back twelve years and he shuddered at the memories, wanting nothing more than to curl up somewhere and hide. A soft hand on his hand and another on his face calmed him, a soft voice saying she loved him whispered in his ear, an equally soft kiss was placed on his cheek, and he slept, the nightmares fading.

Rylee stared down at the man she loved, a question in her eyes. Who had done this? Then she gave an unladylike snort. They were after her, whoever they were, and used Dave as a means of warning and to try and get to her. Caleb had men stationed outside Dave's door. She had also been told that a private security team would be taking over come morning. Her main concern was Dave.

She turned as the door opened and Miriam entered.

"Where's Daniel?"

Miriam smiled at her. "He's gone home to see if he can find Liana. We haven't heard from her. How's Dave?"

"He was stirring a bit ago, but now seems to be asleep."

"Has John said anything?"

Rylee shook her head. "Not yet. He was waiting for results." Rylee turned as the door opened, and Frankie, Caleb and someone she didn't recognize entered.

Frankie spoke to Miriam, then turned to Rylee. "Any word on Dave's condition?"

She stared at him, then shook her head. "No, we're still waiting. What news do you have, Frankie?"

"The truck was stolen." He stopped, a smile appearing as she snorted. "I take it that's what you thought? Caleb is concerned enough that he wants to bring in Abe Finlay and his team for protection for you two for now."

Rylee spun to stare at Caleb and Abe, a puzzled look on her face. Miriam watched with interest, not quite sure what was going on.

"Finlay? No, that's not it." Her eyes focused past the three men watching her. "Lord, it's on the tip of my tongue, isn't it and I just can't get it out?" She spun to pace, the men exchanging puzzled glances. Frankie had a faint smile on his face as he watched. "What was it now, Lord, who was it that Da used to mention? It's one of the times You'll have to hit me over the head to get me to remember. I know the name, but I just can't find it in my memory." She spun to face the men again, her eyes focusing on Abe. "No, not Finlay, is it, Lord? Finlayson. That's it. I'd be thanking You, Lord." She turned to Frankie. "The name I was trying to come up with for you the other day? It's Adam Finlayson and then there's Oscar Finamore. Try those. Dad mentioned them in passing one day, I don't think he even realized he had said them."

Abe exchanged a glance with Caleb, not quite sure what he was getting into.

Rylee spun once more to face Miriam, giving her a wink the men couldn't see. Miriam choked back her laughter. Oh, she could see how much fun it was going to be having Rylee in their lives. A movement from Dave had Rylee at his side, watching as he settled back down.

Caleb spoke finally, over his shock with how she talked to the Lord. "Rylee, we need to do something to keep you safe. Today proved how far they'll go to get to you."

"And are you sure it was me they were trying to get at through Dave?"

Caleb shook his head at her direct glance. "No, we're not, but we're not prepared to take any chances."

Rylee sighed, her eyes raising to the ceiling as she once more communed in silence with her Lord. She brought her eyes back down. "I'd be saying no to any protection, Caleb. It just can't be done. Leave the protection with Dave, if you would, but I can't live like that."

"And you may not, if you don't," Abe finally spoke, bringing her gaze to him.

"I hear what you're not saying, Mr. Finlay, but I can't do it. Put your security on Dave, on my Gran, on Miriam and Daniel, on Donovan and Fergus, but not me. It's just not possible to protect me."

She turned, pacing around, then abruptly pulled the door open and was out through it before the men could react.

"Did she really just do that?" Frankie headed after her.

"Frankie, hold on." Abe shared a look with Caleb. "She's right, you know. We can't keep an eye on her all the time. Joseph was heading in to look over the security system at their home and bakery."

Frankie turned, catching a look on Miriam's face. "Miriam, what do you say?"

"I would like to see her agree, but she's right. She grew up, running the streets of Belfast. She's told me she knows more ways to protect herself that you could even imagine. Trust her. If she wants protection, she'll ask for it."

Caleb nodded. "That's true. She has a different background to us. She won't welcome being caged." He sighed. "Somehow, Abe, that sounds like all the ladies of your guys."

Abe started to laugh, just as Rylee walked back in, drawing a frown from her. "Sorry, Rylee. Caleb just pointed out a fact that is way too obvious."

"Glad he could do that. Now, if you have nothing more for me, may I suggest you convene your meeting somewhere else? The nurse is heading this way as is the doctor."

Miriam gasped as the men started laughing.

"We'll go, Rylee, but we're not done this conversation." Frankie shook his head as he walked by her, missing her wink at Abe, who had to choke back more laughter.

Yes, sir, Dave, he thought, you have a live one there. She's putting us off until she can figure out how to live and still be protected.

The physician entered and headed for Dave's side. "Has he been awake?" He turned to look at the two women.

"Just roused somewhat, but not fully awake." Rylee stood close to the bed, waiting for the doctor's assessment.

"You're his fiancee?" He briefly looked up to catch her nod. "We have good news. Nothing broken. No muscles or tendons torn. Just a lot of deep bruising. I don't suspect he has a concussion but he may have a mild one. He seems to be just sleeping now, so hopefully he'll be awake by tomorrow morning. I would suggest you ladies go home and get some sleep."

"Miriam's going to go when Daniel gets back, but I'll not be leaving his side, not until he's ready to leave."

The physician looked up in protest, then stopped, nodding. "That's fine. I'll be back in the morning. The nurses will be in and out over the night checking on him."

Chapter 11

Grimacing with pain, Dave lowered himself into the recliner at his parents. All had decided he needed to be there until he healed some. Shaking his head at the question on his father's face, he laid his head back, closing his eyes. It had been three days since he had been hit, and the pain seemed worse today.

A soft hand on his face roused him. Rylee perched on the arm of his chair, her hand on the back of his neck.

"Can I get you anything, Dave?"

He again shook his head. "No, it's okay, Rylee. I'm just glad to be home. What day is it, anyway?"

"It's Monday." She watched with concern as emotions flitted across his face.

"And our wedding is coming up on Saturday."

She hushed him with a kiss. "We'll take it a day at a time, Dave. That's all we can do. It's only our families that know the date. They think we should wait a couple of weeks until you're healed."

Dave looked around her as he heard voices in the hall, then groaned. Frankie was here and he really didn't want to speak with him.

"Dave. Rylee." Frankie assessed the couple in front of him. "How are you feeling, Dave?"

"About what you'd expect, Frankie. Do you have any news for us?"

Frankie nodded. "We found the truck, but no luck there." He stared at Rylee for a moment. "Those two names, Rylee, where did you get them?"

Rylee stared back at him with narrowed eyes. "I told you when I gave them to you where I got them. Obviously, you don't believe me. I'm done with this conversation." She was up and gone before Dave could stop her.

Dave turned hard, searching eyes on Frankie. "Care to explain what that was about, Frankie? I won't have you casting any doubt on Rylee."

Frankie nodded. "I wasn't meaning to, Dave. She gave us a couple of names that have come back with ties to a theft ring. We have evidence they are here in town."

"In Riverville?" Dave sat back, astonished. "How does that fit with Rylee?"

"That's what I was wanting to ask her. She said her father mentioned them one day, she thought without even realizing he had." He looked towards the door Rylee had disappeared through. "Any chance she'll come back?"

Dave levered himself to his feet. "I'll see if she will. But you need to remember one thing, Frankie. She grew up different from us, a different way of life. She's been hiding things for a while now, tucked way down inside her because they hurt too much. This is likely one of those."

Rylee looked up from the counter she had been staring at as Dave wrapped an arm around her. "Dave, you shouldn't be up."

Dave's finger touched her lips. "I need to move around more than I've been doing. I stiffen up too much if I sit still for long. Listen, Frankie really needs to talk with you. Sometimes, he doesn't phrase what he wants to ask in the best way. Relics of his days as an undercover cop I would imagine. He's asked if you would come back and talk to him."

She studied Dave's face for the longest time, then finally nodded. "Only if he's more polite in how he phrases things." She looked past him as someone entered the kitchen, a man she didn't recognize.

Dave caught the look on her face and turned. "Joseph, good to see you. I take it you're here to see about Dad's security as well."

Joseph, the security expert on Abe's team, nodded. "I am. Your Dad asked me to." He looked at Rylee. "And this would be Rylee, would it, Dave?"

Dave nodded, making the introductions. "You've finished at Rylee's and the bake shop?"

Joseph nodded. "I have. I've left all the information with her grandmother." He looked behind him. "What's with Frankie? He's pacing."

Rylee snorted, drawing Joseph's eyes to her. "Serves him right." She brushed past the two men.

Dave waited, letting Frankie speak with Rylee on her own. When voices became raised, he headed for the living room, finding Rylee facing down Frankie.

"I have no idea, Frankie. Da never said who they were. I can tell you don't believe me." She raised her eyes to Dave. "I need to leave, Dave. If you talk to your police chief, ask for someone else to talk to me. I'm done."

Rylee was gone before they could stop her. Joseph nodded at Dave and followed her.

Dave turned to Frankie. "What happened, Frankie?"

Frankie's hands went up in the air. "I have no idea, Dave. All I did was ask if she knew anything more about those two men, or any other men her father might have mentioned. She took offence when I mentioned they were thieves and we were looking for any cohorts of them."

Dave shook his head. "This isn't a good week for this, Frankie. She's really missing her parents now that we're planning our wedding. Her emotions are raw and right near the surface."

Frankie's eyes slid shut. "I didn't help that out, did I?"

Dave watched his friend, then spoke. "I have no idea how you're even going to be able to talk with her again, Frankie. I can try and calm her down, but don't expect me to succeed very well. It's not the first time you two have had words."

Frankie nodded. "I know, and I regret that." He paced. "The thing of it is, Dave, we've had word this group is planning something in the area, and we're attempting to determine what it is and stop it. Rylee may be the key to that."

"I doubt that, Frankie. It's too remote for that to be true."

Frankie stared at Dave for a minute. "Just see if she'll at least talk to Caleb? Eddie still off sick." Eddie Brown, senior detective on the force, had been sidelined by a sudden illness a few weeks previous. "I just wish he could talk to her."

"Why don't we talk to Caleb first?"

Frankie agreed. "Just so you know, she's refused Abe's security."

"I figured she would. She won't put anyone at risk if she can help it."

"But that's the thing, Dave. She might be putting the whole city at risk by refusing to talk with me."

"Not likely, Frankie." Dave stared at the door as Frankie closed it, then sighed. He wasn't up to moving around a lot, but he knew he had to go find Rylee.

Joseph walked through the door, looking behind him. "Your lady's sitting in her car, Dave. She never left. I think she was waiting for Frankie to leave."

Dave searched his face, looking for an answer he wasn't sure he wanted to see. "They really don't get along, do they?"

Joseph grinned. "No, they don't. Unfortunately, Frankie has that effect on some people. Abe went through it with Emma and Frankie."

"He did?" Dave headed for the door, Joseph right behind him. "Did you say you had everything set for Rylee?"

"I do." Joseph stopped, staring where her car had been. "She's gone, Dave. She was right there."

Dave nodded. "I quite expected that. Her emotions are really up and down and raw right now. Frankie pushing hasn't helped."

*****

Rylee turned as Donovan approached her in the backyard.

"What's going on, Rylee? You're not acting like yourself."

She shrugged. "I just wish Mam and Da were here right now, that's all. Frankie pushing me isn't helping either."

"He still trying to get you to remember more names?"

She nodded, her eyes on her brother. "And I can't. Those are the only ones I know Da mentioned, and why he did, I have no idea."

Donovan nodded, his eyes moving past her to Fergus who was headed their way.

"Rylee, this package was on the front step for you. It just has your first name on it, no address, no return address."

Rylee had turned to face her brother. "Fergus, please set it down on the ground." She reached for her phone. "I'm not really happy with Frankie right now, but he needs to know about this."

Frankie watched as the crime scene tech processed the box and then opened it. He moved forward as the tech turned to him, stared into the box, then turned to find Rylee. Walking towards her, he watched as her brothers moved in closer to her. The only one missing is Dave, and there is he, Frankie thought, right on schedule.

"Frankie?" Rylee's voice was low.

"Rylee, how be we go somewhere we can sit? The tech will finish processing the box, and then he'll forward some pictures to me."

She shook her head. "Before we go anywhere, talk to me. What is in it?" She pointed to the box.

Frankie stared past her, then brought his eyes first to Dave, then to her. "Okay, then." He really didn't want to be the one to tell her. "There's a picture I believe may be your father and mother on a boat." He reached for her as she shrank back and stumbled, Dave reaching her first.

Her brothers stared at Frankie, then at Rylee. "What's going on here, Rylee?" Fergus faced his sister. "It's more than what you'd be telling us, what with the security upgrades, Dave, and now this."

Rylee kept shaking her head, her whole body trembling. Dave caught her up in his arms, ignoring the pain it brought him, and headed for the house, the three men on his heels. Ailynne took one look at Dave, then pointed for the office.

"In there, Dave. Sit on the couch with her." She followed, a soft throw in her hands that she tucked around the two of them. "And what would have been happening, Dave? I've only seen this once before with her, the day her parents died."

Dave sat, Rylee wrapped in his arms, and waited until she had roused. Quiet words were spoken between them, and then Dave rose to leave, praying that Rylee would see solace in God that night.

Chapter 12

Frankie was on a hunt for Caleb. He had photos from the items in the box and he didn't like what he was seeing, not one bit. Lord, he prayed, help us to solve this before anyone else gets hurt. I can feel the clock ticking down on something, and I have no idea what we're facing.

Caleb looked up from his fax machine as Frankie tapped at his door.

"Got a moment or two, Caleb?"

Caleb nodded and pointed at a chair. "What do you have for me, Frankie?"

Frankie sank down gratefully. It had been a long day and was far from over. "I already know you're not going to like what I have to say."

"That bad?" Caleb tidied the sheets of paper he had in his hand and set them down. "What do you have?"

"There was a box on Rylee's front porch today. She had the sense to call in before it was opened." Frankie stared at the paperwork he held, then handed it over. "This is what we found."

Caleb took it, his eyes studying his friend. "This is wearing you out again, Frankie. Still having trouble getting Rylee to talk to you?"

Frankie nodded. "I am. She's very strong willed and knows her own mind. Dave's working with her to try and get her to cooperate with me."

Caleb opened his mouth to speak, when he glanced down at the photos, stilling as he did so. "This is from Eagle Lake, isn't it?"

"That's what I thought. That's Rylee's parents, but they weren't found on Eagle Lake. They were found in Oak Lake. The tech thinks it's a dummied up photo. But it's the other documents that are concerning."

"How so?" Caleb started flipping through the pages, stopping when he came to the last one. "This is a direct threat at Rylee, now isn't it?"

Frankie agreed. "Dave's aware of it. Rylee isn't. I think we'll have to tell her brothers as well."

Caleb sat back, silent for a few minutes, lost in thought. "How do we keep her safe, Frankie? It feels like all the other guys and their ladies, doesn't it?" Caleb was getting frustrated.

"I did hear tonight that Rylee is refusing to move her wedding date from this Saturday. Dave's trying to talk her into that, given what's going on."

"This Saturday? I hadn't heard they had actually set a date."

Frankie grinned. "No one is supposed to know, other than their immediate family. I've talked to Abe. He'll make sure that they're covered on Saturday. We need to do that."

Caleb nodded, his mind going back to the documents in his hands. "Somehow, Frankie, I don't think that will work. We're into something really deep here. And I don't think it has to do with terrorism at all. That's likely a story to throw us off." He handed the pages back to Frankie. "Pull in who you need to. Eddie called today. He's cleared to come back next week and is itching to get involved in something. Take those to him and talk to him. Ben Johnson would be another to talk to. He's still on our consultant list. Talk to Jace and Emma at Tracker's as well."

Frankie sighed. "Don't suppose you have a few extra hours in a day, do you?"

Caleb laughed as Frankie left, then sobered. *Rylee, he thought, what have you gotten yourself into? Lord, protect them.*

*****

Dave turned as he heard his name called. Frankie walked towards him. Frankie pointed at Mac's. Once settled in a booth, Dave watched Frankie trying to find the words he needed.

"Spit it out, Frankie." He grinned as Frankie shook his finger at him.

"You're a bundle of wisdom this early in the morning, Dave. How are you feeling, by the way?"

"Much better. Yesterday coming home was rough, but the pain is a lot better today. I'm heading back to my place this afternoon."

"Is that a wise idea?"

"Why not?" Dave watched Frankie, knowing his friend wasn't saying what he meant. "I figure the further away from Mom, Dad and Liana, the safer they'll be."

Frankie just stared at him. "Not necessarily, Dave. They may use them to get to you, and then to Rylee." He sighed, knowing he had to continue and not really wanting to. "The team's had time to go over what was in that box."

Dave waited for Frankie to continue. Long moments passed. "What aren't you saying, Frankie?"

Frankie studied his friend's face once again. How do I tell him, Lord? How do I get through to him what is really going on?

"It's like this, Dave. Rylee's father was involved deeply in something that we're still working through. The Irish authorities aren't talking to us, though, so we can't get any information that way." He stopped, his eyes on his coffee mug. He then looked up. "Those names that Rylee gave me came back as not terrorists but as men that were trying to work their way into the black market here in our country."

"Hold on a moment. What names?" Dave was confused.

"That's right. She did it in your hospital room. Abe being there triggered a memory with his last name." He started to laugh. "She really threw Caleb and Abe when she started her praying."

Dave grinned. "She has that effect on people when she does that, but that's the way we should be, isn't it?" He paused, then continued, "She's taught me to pray that way. With that, I sometimes feel like the woman in the Bible who reached out to touch the hem of Christ's garment and was healed."

Frankie nodded. "It's too true, isn't it?" He stared out the window for a moment, making a decision. "I'm letting you in on what we've found so far, Dave. I've talked to Eddie and Ben both. Eddie's back next week, so that will help. You know about the photo? We think it was dummied up as the lake in the background is not the lake they were found in."

"It's not?" Dave was surprised.

"No, it's not. We've pulled the medical examiner's report. Interestingly,

DNA testing was done. Her father had it in his will that if he was found dead in suspicious circumstances, DNA testing was to be done.

"Then, there are other photos of Rylee and her brothers over the past fourteen years since their parents died. Someone has been watching them for that long."

Dave sat back, shocked at that. "Fourteen years? How?"

Frankie shook his head. "We have no idea.   But there's a variety of activities. There's one in particular I found very interesting." He pulled out his phone, pulled up a picture, and handed the phone to Dave.

Dave took it, staring at the photo. "Wait a minute. That's the night we met, and she was accosted."

Frankie sat forward. "What do you mean? We don't have that on file."

Dave looked up, then pulled out his own phone. "Rylee was approached by a man she had noted at the ballgame. She took a picture of him for some reason, she's not even sure why.   She was walking towards the parking lot when he approached her and roughed her up. I tackled him, but he got away. Emma's had a look at him and warned me about him." He sent the photo to Frankie's email. "He wanted her camera and she had forgotten it where we were sitting. I tried to get her to report it, but she refused."

"That figures. Maybe this wouldn't have happened if she had."

"It would have, Frankie. There's been a chain of events in process for years, and we're nearing the end of it. Just how do we stay safe though? They've proved they'll go after whoever is close to her. They've gone after one of her brothers as well."

Frankie sighed. "I wish people would report these kinds of things."

"What else was there? You're not saying everything, Frankie."

"No, I'm not." He hesitated, knowing it would hurt his friend. "They've threatened to kill her if she doesn't provide the information they're looking for."

"And you didn't think it was necessary to warn her?" Dave had to control his emotions. "What information are they looking for?"

"They weren't specific in that. I need to talk to Rylee again, and I need her not to walk away. Eddie and Ben are working on this aspect, but they both feel Rylee has hidden something deep inside, that's too painful to come to the surface. There's also the fact I hear you two have set a wedding date."

Dave sighed. "We have, but we're still debating that." He looked up, catching a look on his friend's face. "What did you do, Frankie?"

Frankie grinned. "Spoke with Abe, so he'll be speaking with you. They want to provide some security for you. I hear tell Lydia's Ian is prepared to fly you two somewhere safe."

Dave laughed, shaking his head. "I don't think Ian will change, now will he? They should never have a daughter. He'd be flying her away to hide once she became a teenager."

Frankie started to laugh at that. "That's exactly what he'd to." Then he sobered. "We need to get to the bottom of this sooner than later."

Dave looked past him and then stood. "Sooner, I think, Frankie." He greeted Rylee with a kiss, then waited until she sat before he sat beside her, claiming her hand. "What brings you here?"

She shrugged, uncertainty on her face. "I'm not sure, Dave. I was looking for you, and the good Lord told me to come here." She faced Frankie. "I know there's a lot more in that box than you told me. Spit it out now, would you?"

Dave choked back a laugh at the look on Frankie's face. Rylee, you do my heart good. Thank you, Lord, for this precious lady. You've brought some healing into my life through her.

Frankie stared at her. "How did you know?"

She stared at him. "Now, were you really thinking I didn't know there was more than what you said in that box? I'm not stupid, Frankie. I know that box was too big to hold just a photo."

Frankie sighed. "Then, I guess we'll need to go find the conference room at the department. We have people working on that as well as the names you gave us. Have you remembered any more names?"

She shook her head. "No, and neither has Gran. I want this over, Frankie. I want my life back. I'm leaving too much of the bake shop to Gran right now."

Chapter 13

Rylee rubbed her hands up and down her arms. Dave watched her, then wrapped her in a hug. She sighed, hating what this was doing to them.

"Can we end this now, Dave? I so want to get on with life."

"Soon, I suspect, sweetheart. Just remember that God is in control of it all." He looked around as he felt someone behind him.

Eddie Brown stood there, watching the two of them.

"Dave?"

Dave turned, hand outstretched. "Good to see you back up on your feet, Eddie."

"It's good to be back, but I didn't expect to get thrown into a case involving you. And who would be this you're holding on to so tight?" Eddie had a sparkle of mischief in his eye.

Dave grinned at him, used to his teasing. "This would be Rylee O'Shea, Eddie. Rylee, this is Eddie Brown, senior detective here, just back from sick leave."

"Rylee O'Shea, is it? Who's in your bake shop if you're here?"

"My Granny and a couple of friends. Donovan is helping out as he can."

Eddie nodded, then looked around. "There's a lot of activity going on here, Rylee. How be we have a seat? Frankie's asked me to talk to you. He seems to think that maybe my gray hairs will find something he's missed."

Dave laughed. "That's possible, Eddie. I hear he's been talking to Ben as well." Dave stopped, knowing that Michael had talked to Ben. Had Ben talked about that to Eddie, he wondered?

Rylee sat, her hand in Dave's, watching quietly as Eddie seated himself and pulled a file over, opening it to glance through it.

Eddie looked up, his keen eyes studying her, not saying anything. Dave knew he would be in prayer before he started talking to her. Eddie sat back, staring past them, then looked back at the folder. They watched as he stood and paced away, lost in thought, then returned to sit once again.

"Rylee, you've lived in this town for how long?"

"I was twelve when we moved here, so eighteen years or so."

"That means your brothers were quite young, doesn't it?" At her nod, he then asked, "How long ago was it you lost your parents?"

"Fourteen years." Dave could see she was puzzled by how Eddie had started the conversation.

"Had your father ever talked about going back to Ireland?"

She shook her head. "Gran asked him one day if he would, and he said he never would, that where we were was home. There was a sadness in his voice when he said that. It was after that he mentioned those two names. I don't think he realized he had."

"Did you ever know what your father did for a living?"

She was genuinely puzzled. "What do you mean? He was a businessman and set up his business here. It was something international, I think. He just never talked about what he did, nor did Mam."

Dave sensed that Eddie was coming closer to what he wanted to ask. "Rylee, did your Mom ever say anything?"

She looked at Dave as she shook her head. "Never. And now that you mention it, that's strange. My friends and their parents always talked about what they did, but mine never did." She looked at the men, concern colouring her face. "He wouldn't have been doing something illegal, now would he?"

Eddie shook his head. "Rest assured, Rylee, your father was an honourable upright man. In fact, his business was trying to bring lawbreakers to justice." He looked back down at the folder and made a decision. He closed it and handed it to her. "This is what we've found out about your parents. Read it, then come find me. I'll be around here somewhere."

Rylee looked down at the folder, a pensive look on her face. "The boys should be here, Dave. They need to hear and see this. It's not the same as me telling them this."

Dave agreed. Dropping a kiss on her cheek, he rose and went to find Eddie.

Fergus and Donovan approached their sister, caution in their movements, and then seated themselves, one on either side of her. Dave stood behind her, hands on her shoulders.

"Rylee, what's going on? Why are we here?" Fergus was visibly upset. "No one would tell us why."

Rylee reached for her brothers' hands. "They've found some information on Da, and I wanted to see it first with you two. You were both so young when they went." Rylee bit her lip, fighting back tears as Dave's hands tightened on her shoulders.

Donovan nodded, then looked at Fergus. "This is one of those times Da always say pray first, then go forward."

"Dave, would you?" Rylee turned to look back at him.

Dave prayed for wisdom and understanding for what they would be looking at, for strength and courage and protection on what they would face. He felt himself that they were just entering the hardest part of the whole trouble, that they had no idea what they would be facing.

Rylee took a deep breath and opened the folder, her brothers leaning close. As they leafed through the photos and copies of the documents, Rylee sat back, staring ahead.

"Dave, is there somewhere that's a bit quieter, do you think? Somewhere we can lay all these out and look at them as a larger picture? And I would like highlighters and red pens and those sticky notes if I can."

"Let me find Eddie and see what we can arrange for you."

Dave turned to find Eddie standing behind him, watching them. Eddie motioned for them to follow, leaving them in a smaller board room. He was back with what Rylee had requested.

Watching as she worked, Dave could see the puzzlement on the siblings' faces on what they were seeing.

Donovan finally picked up the first photo. "There's something off here about Mam and Da, Fergus, but I can't figure out what it is."

"I thought that too, Donovan. Rylee, did you pick up on anything?"

She turned, bringing her thoughts back to her brothers. "I know, but I can't think of what it is." She took the photo and studied it, finally pointing to an area. "Dave, can we get this enlarged, do you think? This is what is throwing us off."

Dave took the photo and studied it. "I can tell what it is. That's a marker buoy that shouldn't be on the lake they were found on. It's from a different lake." Dave looked up at Rylee's gasp. "Rylee?"

"That's what it's been then. That's what I could never figure out. Why were they even out on a lake? Mam hated water, was terrified of it in fact." She reached for the photo again. "They're not on a boat in this picture, are they?"

Fergus reached for it. "I know this photo. When you say it's not on a lake, you're right. It was taken back in Ireland, near our old home."

The three siblings stared at each other. What had their father been involved in?

Eddie stood in the doorway, a perplexed look on his face. What had Rylee discovered that they had missed? He headed towards them.

"Time for a break. Mac sent in your favourites."

Donovan reached for the bags. "How does he do that, Eddie? How does he know what we like and remember it?"

Eddie shrugged. "I've known Mac all my life. He's always been like that. He says it's his gift from God, hospitality."

Rylee reached for the grilled chicken salad she had been sent. "I don't care how he does it. Gift or not, I intend to enjoy his food." Her levity broke up the solemnity of the morning.

Eddie reached for his own dinner and then asked the blessing on their meal. He waited until they were almost finished, listening to Dave gently tease all three of the O'Sheas, bringing a release of tension and smiles to their faces. Lord, You blessed Dave with this gift of being able to help people through laughter and joy. Thank you. We needed this today. Dave likes to tease, but he's sensitive with it.

"So, Rylee, tell me what you have." Eddie didn't look right at her, but didn't miss the start she gave when he spoke.

She studied his face, then nodded. "There's something about Mam and Da." She started to rise but stayed sitting as Dave laid a hand on her shoulder.

"I'll get it, Rylee. Anything else you need from there?"

She thought about it, then shook her head. "Just that photo for now."

Dave handed it to her, then sat back down. "What is it that's off?"

She stared at him, lost in thought. Then she studied the picture once again. "It's their clothes. The clothes are what they wore back home, not here. Mam's hair was longer than it was when she died. She used to wear it back in a braid or curled up in a bun. She had been quite ill with a high fever about six months before she died and had had to cut her hair short. It just about broke her heart." She smiled at a memory. "Da used to steal the band she'd have on the end of the braid."

Fergus reached for the picture. He had been only 12 when his parents died, but he had memories of those days. "You're right, Rylee." Then he studied the background. "This looks like a stock photo of the lake. It's not even the right time of year. We lost them in the fall. This looks like late spring."

Eddie reached for the picture, his eyes meeting Dave's. With all their looking, both he and Frankie had missed that it was a different time of year. "You three are good, you know. You've picked up on something we missed. What else?"

Fergus stood, going back to look over the documents again, finally picking up one.

"This. It says it's Da's birth certificate, but the names are wrong."

Rylee reached for it. "You're right, Fergus. Mam's name is spelled differently that it should be on this certificate. Gran has their original wedding certificate locked away. And Da's date of birth on the other one is wrong." She was up and over to the table, picking up another page.

She stopped, freezing in place as she once again looked at the photos spread out. Hand to her mouth, she slowly reached for one. Tears close to the surface, she turned towards Dave, who had been by her side.

"What is it, Rylee?"

"This. This is wrong. Mam and Da were high school sweethearts. They married before they went to college. I'm their oldest. There is no older child." She poked at the photo she held. "This tries to say there's an older child."

Donovan and Fergus spun around at her words, and Eddie rose and came towards her.

"Rylee?" Dave tried to catch her attention, but she was focused on the photo.

She spun and headed for the door, Dave reaching it before her and preventing her from leaving.

"Rylee? Talk to me. Then, I'll take you where you want to go."

Rylee stared at the door. "I need to go home, Dave. I need to find something there."

A movement from Eddie caught his attention.

"We'll get you there, Rylee, but you're not going on your own. I want to send officers with you." Eddie was adamant that she was not leaving on her own.

She finally nodded and moved to let Eddie leave.

Chapter 14

Rylee stared around the office at her home. She knew what she wanted was here, she had seen it just the other day. Now, where was it?

"What are you looking for, Rylee?"

She turned to Dave. "I can't describe it really, Dave. It's a brown mottled metal box. It was Da's."

Dave turned to look as well, finding it at last tucked away on a book shelf. He handed to Rylee, who took the small, thin box, felt its weight and nodded.

"Let's head back, Dave. This should help, I hope."

Dave held her back for a moment, watching her face. "Talk to me, Rylee. What's this about?"

She sighed, then looked down at the box. "It's something that Da had gathered. He told me once never to open it if he was alive, only if he were to die. I have never wanted to open it, afraid of what I'd be finding. Now's the time to do it, I'm guessing." Emotions had thickened her accent again.

Dave reached to pull her into his arms. "Then, that's what you'll do, honour your father by opening it now. Come, they're waiting for us outside." He reached for her hand, then stopped her at the door.

Something was off. The patrol officer was not waiting at the door as he had promised he would.

"Dave?"

"Something's wrong, Rylee." Dave stepped to the side window to watch for the officer but couldn't see him. He reached to set the locks on the door. "The officer isn't there."

He motioned her to be silent and to stay where she was, then walked quietly towards the back of the house, eyes searching for anything off. He reached for his phone.

"Frankie? Dave. Something's off here. The officer isn't at the front of the house."

Frankie spun to find Eddie, motioning him over.

"Can you get more patrols to Rylee? Dave can't see the officer that went with them."

Eddie took one look at Frankie, then ran for the front dispatch, then for his own vehicle, Frankie on his heels going out the back door.

Rylee rubbed her hands up and down her arms, then wrapped her arms around herself, the box clutched tight in one hand. A noise at the door had her clapping a hand over her mouth to stop screaming out loud. Dave's hand on her arm startled her and she spun. His finger to his mouth, he drew her with him.

"We have help on the way. We need to find somewhere to hide until they get here." His voice was low in her ear.

She nodded, then looked at the box in her hand, holding it up for Dave. He nodded, then took it from her, sliding it into his jacket pocket. Another sound at the door had him once again looking around for a hiding spot.

Rylee caught his hand, pulling him with her. She raced up the stairs, heading for the attic, Dave's feet as quiet as they could be on the stairs behind her. She pointed at the far wall. Dave gave her a puzzled look as she tugged him with her. She reached and pulled open a small door, pulling him into the spot behind her.

"Put your phone on vibrate, Dave. I don't know how thick these walls are."

"Where are we?"

"We're above the kitchen. There's a small corridor that leads across the garage and to the far end. That end looks just like an ordinary vent, but we can get down from there. The boys found it not long after we moved in here. Da encouraged them to use it. I don't think they have for a while, though. I had almost forgotten it."

"How do we get down?" He pulled out his phone as it vibrated. "Frankie?"

"Dave, we're outside Rylee's now. The officer is down as you suspected. The patrol officers who responded caught one of the culprits. Now, where are you?"

Dave started to laugh as he sank back down on the floor. "We'll be right back down. I don't think I'm going to tell you."

Rylee shook her head at him as she pushed the door open again. Dave reached for her and drew her into his arms.

"That was too close, Rylee."

She clung to him for a moment, then stepped back. "It was. Now, let's go find Frankie."

Frankie and Eddie watched as the two walked back down the stairs, a puzzled look on both their faces.

Rylee shook her head. "I'm not saying where we were. We could have gotten out, though." She peered around them at the activity outside the house. "What happened?"

"The patrol officer was ambushed from behind. Thank God you two were in the house." Eddie looked between the two of them. "Why didn't you go out?"

Dave shrugged. "Just a feeling, like I used to get when we'd be out of patrol. Something felt off when I got to the door."

Frankie shook his head. He knew Dave had been overseas but Dave never talked much about his tour. To hear this meant Dave was still attuned to the dangers around him. Frankie pointed at the door.

"Let's get you two back to headquarters. Your brothers have found some other interesting discrepancies, Rylee." He stopped, then turned back. "Fergus had an interesting comment."

"And that would be?" Rylee reached for Dave's hand, ready to walk through the door.

"He wondered if you had thought of the photo album from the summer your parents died. He seemed to think there might be something in it."

Rylee stared at Frankie, then Eddie. She was puzzled, but turned back to the living room, reaching for that album. Dave took it from her, then watched as she approached the shelf family photos were centered on. She picked up two photos and then took his hand, heading for the door. Eddie and Frankie exchanged glances and Frankie shrugged. So far he hadn't been able to read Rylee at all like he normally could read his witnesses.

Fergus and Donovan approached Rylee when she entered the boardroom. A quick hug among the three and then she took the album from Dave and handed it to Fergus. She handed the photos to Donovan. A quick quiet word and he was sitting back at a table, pulling off the backs of the frames.

Dave watched the activity, then handed Rylee the box that had started it all. She took it, not moving, just staring at it. She jumped when Dave laid his hands on hers.

"It's what your father wanted, my sweetheart. What was it he would have said to you? 'Open it, lass. It's time.' Is that it?"

Rylee nodded, then brushed the tears from her face. "He always called me lass. It was his pet name for me. Thank you, Dave." She reached up to touch his face, her eyes studying his. "I need you with me when I do. I have no idea what Da has hidden in here."

Rylee set the box on the table and hesitated, her eyes rising to the ceiling.

Dave sat beside her, not saying a word. He knew she was communing with her Heavenly Father.

Finally, she sighed and turned her attention to the box, not realizing that all eyes in the room were on her. Her brothers crowded as close as they could, Dave moving back to let them.   Rylee's eyes searched for him and he went to stand behind her once more, his hands on her shoulders.

"Rylee?"   Fergus' voice was quiet. "What did Da put in there?"

She shrugged.   "I have no idea, Fergus, but his words to me were that I was to open it when he died. Lass, he said, if I'm not here, at some point you'll need what's in here for you and the boys." She bit her lip to keep the tears at bay. "I can hear him so plainly telling me that. It was only about a week before they died."

Donovan's hand laid on her arm. "Do you want us to open it for you, then?"

She shook her head. "No, as the eldest in the family, I need to. You weren't old enough for Da to have said it to."

She drew a deep breath and worked to open the box. Holding the loose lid in her hands, she hesitated, then removed it.

Pulling out the envelope in the box, she felt a hard object in it. She still hesitated, then opened it.

Puzzled, she unfolded the letter, a key dropping from it.

"Dear Children,

"If you are reading this, then I have gone home, leaving my beloved family behind. Do not grieve for me for I am in a much better place. Hold tight to your faith, my loves.

"If you are reading this, then I did not die a natural death. You three did not know what I did to earn the money for our family. No, nothing illegal. I was part of a group of men, businessmen, scholars, law enforcement, government officials, that had formed a group to combat the sale and smuggling of our national treasures, the sale and smuggling of drugs, the sale and smuggling of weapons and armaments, the sale and smuggling of people for labour. I was involved in the first group, our national treasures.

"If you are reading this, then be aware that someone will come after you, looking for the list of where we have found these treasures and the men who had stolen them and the ones who had bought them. I have it hidden well. Rylee, you will be able to figure it out, I'm sure, lass.

"Fergus and Donovan, work with Rylee on this. If you are now adults reading this, know that your Mam and I prayed daily for you all.

"Luv Da."

Rylee and her brothers wrapped their arms around one another for a few minutes, then Rylee reached for the photos. She pulled the frames apart, looking for something. Behind the picture of the five family members, she found a small, folded piece of paper. Unfolding it, she read, then looked for Frankie and Eddie.

"Here, this is where you'll find information. Take this key, it works the box."

Eddie took what she offered, his eyes on her before raising to Dave's. "What is this, Rylee?"

"Da hid valuable information on the ones who killed him in that box. It's been a lot of years, so I'm not sure how valuable it is now." She blinked back tears, her hands gripping her brothers. "Please, tell me you'll search it out and clear Da's name."

"That we will do, Rylee. Thank you." Eddie looked up at Dave and nodded. "Now, what more can you tell me from what is in this room?"

She shrugged. "Nothing more." She stood abruptly. "I need to get out of here, Dave. The boys will want to stay." They nodded as she turned from them and headed for the door, Dave reaching for her hand to stop her.

"Where do you want to go?"

She shrugged once more, eyes staring ahead. "I don't know, Dave. That's the thing. Where do I go where they can't find me? The boys are safe, unless they try to get to me through them and I have no doubt they've already tried that."

Dave drew her back against him, wrapping his arms around her. "Tell you what. Let me call Ian and see if he's free.

Maybe he can take us up in his plane for a while."

She shook her head. "Mam hated water. I hate flying." She turned in his arms, wrapping hers around him. "Take me to our place. I need the quiet there."

Dave nodded. "Okay, then. We'll need someone to take us though."

She sighed. "Forget that. It won't be the same." She then said, "How about the church, then?"

"Okay, we can go there. Greg's usually there, and we really should be talking with him anyway."

Eddie followed them, finding a patrol officer to go with them. Dave led Rylee into the church sanctuary and up to the front row, sitting down beside her and wrapping an arm around her.

"Talk to me, Rylee."

She laid her head on him. "I don't know what's going on any more, Dave. Life seems to have taken on a life of its own. Finding out the truth now seems irrelevant to what we're all feeling."

Dave looked up at quiet footsteps and nodded at their minister, Greg Evans, as he approached, then sat on the stairs near them.

"Greg's here, lass. Maybe he can help us work this through."

Greg searched their faces, then looked up as the patrol officer entered and stood back to the doors. Not another one, Lord, he thought. How much more can our people and my friends take?

Rylee looked up at Greg, her eyes shimmering with unshed tears.

"Greg, why? Why did God allow this?"

Greg nodded. "Fair question, Rylee. One many have asked before you. Just to start, this is about your parents?"

She nodded. "We've had word that they were murdered, and not where they were found. It just seems too much to bear or to even understand."

"A friend of ours would tell you that God has a plan and purpose we don't see or understand and may never do here on earth. I also know that it's often difficult to understand how things can get to this point.

Have you come to the conclusion then that you need to get involved and solve this?"

Rylee shook her head. "I don't want to, Greg, but it seems I'm being involved whether I want to be or not."

Greg watched her closely as she spoke, a prayer unspoken for the wisdom he needed.

"How then can I help you, Rylee? What words can I speak to you?"

She shrugged. "I'd not be knowing that, Greg. If I did, I'd be searching them out myself."

Dave tightened his hold on her. "Rylee is being chased, Greg, just like others of our friends. She's turned over everything she has to the police, but the culprits still seem to think she knows something or has something. They tried to get into her home today when we were there." He looked down at Rylee, seeing the sadness in her face. "She needs healing, Greg, healing for so many hurts."

Greg nodded. "I hear what you're saying, Dave. I think you do too. You've never talked about your time overseas but it affects you each and every day."

Greg paused, reaching for a Bible. "I want to take you to one of my favourite passages on healing. There are many. We know Christ as the Great Physician. Tell me, what do you remember of the story of the woman with the issue of blood? That she suffered with for so many years without being helped? Or do you remember that all she did was touch the hem of the clothing that Christ wore and was instantly healed? I remember both. Just remember, she didn't speak with Christ. She just knew all she had to do was approach Him and touch his garment to be healed. That's all she wanted to do.

"For us, it's a little different but we can still approach Him knowing He will give full healing. He will use medical people, friends, ministers, families. He works through them today. But we have to approach Him and ask."

Rylee's eyes had fastened on Greg as he spoke, not blinking. Then, she sighed. "It sounds so easy, Greg, almost too easy."

He gave a laugh. "We humans think we need to work for everything that God offers freely. That's part of the healing process, Rylee, realizing that God does give without any strings. We still have our part to do, but God doesn't make healing or anything He does contingent on us fulfilling a laundry list of conditions."

Rylee nodded, then looked at Dave. "Greg's right, Dave, and I needed to hear that. I need that touch to the garment right now, and so do my brothers."

Greg held up a hand. "It's up to an individual when and where they do that. We can't do it for someone else. Let me pray with you, Rylee, and you too, Dave."

Chapter 15

Later that night, Dave stood in his kitchen, leaning back on his counter, arms crossed, staring at the wall in front of him. Doug and Abe shared a look, then looked at Dave. Something was up, just what they weren't sure. Doug leaned against the doorframe, feet crossed, hands in his pockets.

"Talk to us, Dave. What's going on?" Doug was concerned about his friend.

When Dave didn't speak, Abe gave a puzzled look at Doug, then spoke. "Dave. We need to help you, but we can't if you don't talk to us. What happened today that's causing you to look like this?"

Dave finally sighed and looked at them. "This is one time I wish I had gone into law enforcement."

"Rylee?" Abe guessed.

Dave nodded and brought them up to date on what all was going on.

"That's a lot to have happened in such a short period of time, Dave, but then that's what happened with us, too." Doug stopped to think. "Frankie and Eddie are working on this?"

"They are. I think they're talking to Emma as well, Abe, to see what she and Jace can dig up."

"Have they talked to anyone in Ireland, yet?"

Dave shrugged. "I have no idea. They're not saying a whole lot. We're hoping what we dug up today will help." He yawned. It had been a long day.

"Listen, we'll go and let you get some sleep, seeing as you're working tomorrow." Doug paused. "If you need us, call."

"I will. Thanks, guys." Dave locked the door after then, then stretched, his muscles still sore but not as painful as they had been.

Lord, he prayed, watch over my lass and her family tonight, please. Keep them safe. Guide those searching for the truth.

*****

Dave pulled his kits from the back of the ambulance and dropped them on the stretcher. He turned to Tom.

"How many times have we made a run here?"

Tom shrugged as he smiled. "I have no idea, but likely once or twice a month. Mrs. Caswell really needs to be somewhere safer."

"That she does. Did dispatch say who called it in?"

Tom started laughing and Dave turned to stare at him. "It was your lady, Dave. Apparently Rylee had stopped by with some sweets for her and found her crumpled on the floor." He sobered. "This time though I don't think Mrs. C. will be heading back home. It sounded as if she had broken a hip."

Dave nodded. Mrs. Caswell had been a staple in town for so many years, teaching music in the elementary schools before retiring and continuing private lessons.

Rylee looked up from where she knelt beside the elderly lady and then smiled in pleasure as she saw Dave. "Here you go,

Mrs. C.   You've got two of the best paramedics to look after you."

Mrs. C. refused to let go of Rylee's hand, her own hand cold and clammy. Rylee was worried. The woman had not answered her door as she usually did, so Rylee had tapped and then entered, finding her collapsed on her kitchen floor.

"Dave Allison, it's you again, is it?" The woman was pleased, smiling through her pain.

"What did you go and do this time, Mrs. C.?" Dave asked gently as both he and Tom began their assessment.

Tom reached to put the oxygen on her, but she pulled the mask back off. Rylee pushed it back gently and kept her hand there.

"She was telling me she slipped this morning when she was getting her morning coffee and tumbled to the floor. That was what, around 7?"

Dave and Tom exchanged a glance. It was now 2 in the afternoon. Although the weather was hot, it was still a long time for an elderly lady to have lain in pain and discomfort. Dave quickly started an IV and then pulled out the heart monitor.

"Now, what are you doing, young man?"

Dave smiled at her. "We just need to check your heart out."

"My heart's just fine. It's yours I'm worried about. Haven't you found a nice young lady yet?" She pointed at his left hand. "I don't see a ring there, Dave Allison."

Dave shot a quick glare at Tom who was doing his best to choke back laughter. Tom wondered how Dave would respond.

Mrs. C. pointed to Rylee. "Now there's a nice young lady, not married yet. At least I don't think so."

"But I'd be spoken for, Mrs. C." Rylee gently placed the oxygen mask back on the patient's face.

"You are?" The oxygen mask went flying back down. "You didn't tell me that. How long? And who is he?"

By this point, Tom had to turn away to control his face. Dave shook his head at him.

"It's okay, Mrs. C. You know him well, I'd be thinking." Rylee shared a smile with Dave. "You see, my intended is the one you're trying to pair me up with."

"Well, why didn't you tell me? Help me up. This calls for a celebration." She moved, and her face whitened with pain. She didn't resist when Rylee pushed the mask back over her nose and mouth.

"We're going to take good care of you. Just let us do our job and we'll have you back on your feet in no time." Dave watched with concern as her face whitened even more.

"I don't think so, not this time, Dave Allison. I had time to commune with my Lord today. It's about time I was going home." Her eyes closed and then her breathing stopped.

Dave and Tom did their best, but their friend had gone. Tom went to call it in as Dave helped Rylee to her feet.

"She was ready, Rylee. She was laughing at the end, taking care of those she cared for."

Rylee nodded through her tears. "She was. She was such a special lady, Dave. I'll miss her."

*****

Dave tapped at Rylee's door later that afternoon. Donovan answered and without a word, pointed towards the back yard. Dave nodded and headed that way, anxious to find Rylee. Dropping down beside her, he wrapped an arm around her.

"She was such a sweet lady, Dave. I'll miss her."

"She was. She cared about everyone who ever crossed her path. I don't think she forget anyone's name."

Rylee sighed. "It's so hard. I don't know how you do your work."

"Days like today are really tough, when you lose a friend. You get through it. God listens to me when I talk to Him about my day and brings me peace. He helps me to deal with what I see."

"Frankie was around." She sounded down, not her usual self.

"He was? What did he have to say?"

"More questions, no answers. They're trying to trace back what I gave them, but it's been too long. He said they might not be able to. And the man they arrested the other night refused to talk and they had to release him when he could come up with his bail money. Frankie wanted to warn us that he was out."

Dave nodded, his chin brushing against her hair. "I thought he would be. How do we do it then? How do we keep you safe?"

She shrugged. "I have no idea, Dave, other than I'm tired of looking over my shoulder, watching cars as they drive by, studying people who walk around me. I've taken to hiding in the kitchen at work, and I miss the people who come in."

Dave hugged her closer, then stood, pulling her to her feet. "Did Frankie say anything else?"

She stopped for a moment, thinking about their conversation, then shook her head. "I don't think they've found out a lot."

Dave's phone chimed at that moment, and he groaned. He prayed it wasn't Ken asking him to cover another shift.

"Emma, this is a surprise."

"Good evening, Dave. Any chance you and Rylee could join Abe and I for dinner tonight, around 6?"

Rylee nodded when Dave relayed the message.

"We'll there. Rylee asked if we could bring anything. No? Okay, we'll see you in a while."

Rylee bit her lip, uncertainty in her manner. Dave watched her, finally turning her face to him.

"What's wrong, sweetheart?"

She shrugged. "Just nerves, I guess. I just realized how big a group of friends you have." Her eyes shone with an emotion he couldn't understand.

"I have, but remember, this is where I've lived all my life."

She nodded. "I know. I miss that. I had lots of friends when I was young. Here, I haven't had a chance to make many."

Dave's heart sank. Here was something he could have worked on for her and he totally missed it. Lord, like Rylee says, this is one time You needed to hit me over the head to get my attention.

"I have friends whose wives meet on a weekly basis on a Thursday night for Bible study. I know you'd be welcome to join them. One of them is my cousin, Lydia, Ian's wife."

She turned back to him. "Why, Dave?"

"Why what? Why ask you to join them? Why ask if they'll welcome you? Because you need that friendship and support."

She sighed. "I guess you're right. I've gotten used to it just being the boys and Gran."

He wrapped an arm around her to lead her back to the house, his eyes searching the area around them. He could feel the evil, could feel the eyes watching them, and he wanted her inside where she might be a little safer.

"I'll need to change, Dave, if we're going out to dinner."

Dave stopped her, realizing how uncertain she had become, not his confident Rylee. "Let me put it this way, Rylee. Whatever you choose to wear, it won't matter. It's you they want to see. Knowing Emma, she's just as apt to be in her worn T-shirt and faded jeans as in anything else, with one of Abe's plaid shirts on as a jacket."

"Really? Somehow, that's not how I picture her."

"It's her. She used to have a lot of money but gave it all way. She's gotten used to wearing those types of clothes. Jeans and a T-shirt or sweater is fine."

*****

Rylee stood watching as Abe and Dave joked with one another, then turned as Emma approached her, little Isaac Peter in her arms. Rylee was surprised when she was handed the baby, but watched as Emma turned to finish their meal.

"Nervous, Rylee?" Emma had her back to her, a slight smile on her face.

"Yes. But why, I have no idea?"

Emma turned, her keen gray eyes watching her friend as she now considered her. "You've been going through a lot lately. I understand that.   I also understand that emotions are running high for you and your brothers as well." She paused, watching as Rylee's eyes slid closed over her tears. "If you need to cry, Rylee, go ahead. I've done it so many times over the years, when no one could see or hear me. Don't let that happen to you." She turned to look at the two men. "Dave's been through a lot, but he's strong. He jokes and teases but he has a heart of gold and a soft one at that underneath it all. He's able to absorb any tear or any emotion that you throw at him." She sighed. "But then, just like all the guys in our lives, he'll want to make it all better for you.   Sometimes, that just isn't possible."

Rylee nodded, surprised at Emma's candor, then wondered how she had gotten so wise.

Emma was watching Rylee's face. Lord, she's hurting so bad and trying to cover it up. Heal her. Let her touch the hem of Your garment.

"Do you know my story?" Rylee shook her head at Emma's question.

Emma pointed at the living room. "Go on in and have a seat. I'll bring in your tea. Dinner will be another twenty minutes or so."

Rylee watched as Emma curled up in Abe's favourite chair. She wondered what story Emma might have to tell. She was so relaxed and confident in her life.

"Rylee, our friends know our story, most of it anyway. Abe and I were college sweethearts and married about a month before college ended, not telling anyone. I had trust funds that I wanted to transfer away from my aunt's husband so he couldn't get his hands on them. When I went home after graduation to pack my things, he drugged me and then led me to believe Abe had been killed in an accident. I ran, with some help. For ten years, I lived with that knowledge, just a shell of myself. A friend and I started up Tracker's. A while ago, Abe happened to walk into the office. He had been told I didn't want anything to do with him and was finally beaten and dumped somewhere to be left to die."

Rylee's hand was at her mouth. "Emma, you would never know."

Emma nodded, her eyes softening as she watched her son grasp for Rylee's hair and Rylee gently remove it. She made a decision to share something only Abe knew about.

"I had reason to hate the man, but I chose not to. When Abe and I reunited and set out on our adventure of marriage, we determined to bring the man down. We were able to finally, but not without a lot of danger and hurt to both of us." She paused, her eyes glistening for a minute with tears. "Only Abe knows what I am about to tell you, other than our physician. What we didn't know at the time was that I was expecting our first child. The trauma I went through and the drugs used meant I lost that little one, despite the efforts of the doctors Jace's mom brought in."

"Oh, Emma. That's so sad." Rylee's tears dripped and she reached to brush them away.

Emma nodded. "We've had to deal with many things over the past few months, but we both agreed that was the hardest one. God has been gracious, Rylee. He truly is the Great Physician. He'll be there with you no matter what you go through. I know it's not over for you, not by a long shot. With you, you're not part of the investigation like Abe was."

Dave and Abe had entered the kitchen and stopped as they heard the women talking. Dave turned to his friend, shock and sorrow on his face for what Abe had lost. Abe nodded, a brief flicker of sorrow and pain crossing his face.

Dave drew a deep breath, then spoke. "Abe, I'm sorry. How do we help you?"

Abe shrugged. "We've worked through it, most days. Now, let's get our ladies and then see what we can do for you two."

Abe made suggestions as to what they could or couldn't do to help find the men. Dave agreed with most of them, but one he was adamant he won't try. There was no way Rylee was going to put herself out there as a target.

Chapter 16

Dave watched through the windshield at the driving rain. A severe storm had moved in and they were reporting to one of dozens of motor vehicle accidents. He hated it when it was raining this hard. It was so difficult to work when they could hardly see.

Tom slowed and stopped, his rain gear sounding as he moved.

"Where's the vehicle. Dave? This is where we were told to find it."

"I know. I don't see anything. They said it was a two car accident. Drive forward a bit more, Tom." Dave reached for the radio, asking for more information and letting dispatch know there were no vehicles there.

"There's nothing, Dave."

Dave nodded. "A setup in the rain, Tom. That's what it was. Let's go." He reported their availability. Dave shot a look at Tom when he was informed that Frankie wanted to speak with him.

"Where will we find him?"

"Mac's." The female dispatcher's voice was steady, although she had been dealing with multiple incidents over the last few hours. "You're on break as of now."

Dave shook the rain off his slicker, then slid out of it, heading for the booth at the back, Tom at his heels. Frankie was waiting for them. Dave hesitated a moment as he saw Michael there as well and caught the slight shake of Michael's head. Okay, Lord, so what's up, Dave asked? Michael doesn't want me to let on we've talked, so I guess we don't. Lead us to the truth, Lord.

Frankie waited until Mac had brought their meals, then spoke, "Dave, what happened out there today?"

"What do you mean? That we were called to an accident that wasn't there?"

Frankie nodded. "That's what. Michael here reported to me that he overheard some men plotting this to try and get to you." He searched Dave's face, then Tom's. "Why didn't you get out?"

Tom and Dave shared a look, then Tom spoke. "We didn't see any vehicles and it was to have been a two-car accident. Dave felt something, didn't you, Dave?"

Dave nodded. "I did. It's like when we would go out on patrol. We always knew when it was the most dangerous, we could feel it. I had a similar feeling today."

Frankie nodded. He knew those feelings only too well.

A sudden loud boom and rattling of the windows startled all the patrons. The four men were on their feet and headed for the door.

Dave and Tom's radios crackled to life, and they paused to stare at each other. An explosion in a building down town. Dave's heart sank. Please don't let it be the Irish Charm.

Frankie headed for his vehicle, stopping as he heard the address. No, Lord, please not that. He changed directions and ran for Dave.

"Dave! Wait up!"

Dave jerked to a halt and turned as he heard Frankie's voice. "What is it, Frankie?"

"It was a bomb, they think, in a building near Rylee's."

Dave paled and then turned to run even quicker for his ambulance, Tom sliding behind the wheel. Frankie was right behind them as they left, sirens and lights going.

Michael stood and watched, his heart in his mouth. Had they gotten to Rylee after all, he wondered? He turned at a touch on his arm. Mac motioned him back into the cafe.

"You used to work for me at times, Michael. Let's put your old skills to work."

Michael nodded, heading after Mac.

Mac studied Michael, then finally spoke. "You're not here to visit family, are you, Michael?"

Michael shot him a glance, then looked at the activity surrounding him. "Not really, Mac, but I can't say much about it."

Mac nodded. "I understand. If you have something that can help Dave's Rylee and need someone to get it to Frankie or Eddie, let me know." Mac walked away at that point, Michael staring after him, finally closing his mouth. He shook his head. How did Mac do that, he wondered?

*****

Dave and Tom were forced to wait on the sidelines as the fire crews searched the rubble of the buildings.

"Was Rylee's one of them, Dave?"

Dave squinted through the rain. "It doesn't look like it." He looked up as he heard his name called, then moved towards the fire captain.

"We have a couple of victims here, Dave. They're alive, thankfully."

"Any other causalities yet?" Tom voiced the question in both their minds.

The man shook his head. "So far, it looks as if the buildings were empty, which is strange for this time of day."

"So, someone warned them and got them out?"

"That's what we're thinking, Dave." He pointed to where his crews were working. "Right there."

*****

Dave moved slowly at the end of the day. It was long past time they should have ended their shift, but hadn't been able to. Thank You, Lord, that we only had those two hurt, and not that bad at all. I don't know who warned the people, but thank You that someone did.

He paused before he walked up to Rylee's door. He was exhausted but wanted to see his lady before heading home. He just had to make sure she was safe.

"Dave?" He heard a voice from their porch.

"Donovan, what are you doing out here?"

"Waiting for you. Rylee won't tell you herself, but she's the one who warned the people today."

"Rylee? How? Is she okay?" Dave climbed the stairs to the porch and faced Donovan.

"She is, but it really took a toll on her. She was putting stuff in the dumpster, saw a box that was out of place, she said. She just went through the buildings, told everyone to get out, that something wasn't right. They all made it out just before the bomb went off."

"Was it at the bakeshop?"

Donovan shook his head. "That's the thing, Dave. If it had been, Rylee wouldn't have been able to get out the back door. It was down at the photographer's."

Dave froze. "Has she talked to Frankie or Eddie?"

Donovan nodded. "She called them as soon as she had been through the buildings. But why the photographer's?"

"Did your parents ever use that place to develop pictures?"

Donovan shook his head. "Da always did his own developing. We still have the dark room set up, just got rid of all the chemicals."

Dave drew a sigh of relief. "So, that's not the reason. At least, I don't think so." He looked towards the door. "Is Rylee inside?"

"Try the back yard. She was headed there after supper. She has a bench near the back she likes to sit in."

"It's dark. And I bet the bench is well sheltered."

Donovan spun around at Dave's words, and his eyes slid shut. "It is. We're just so used to being safe, we never thought."

Dave headed with quick steps for the back yard, praying that Rylee was safe. As he approached the bench, he saw her sitting there, knees drawn up and arms wrapped around them, chin down on them. She looked up as he approached.

Dave dropped to the bench beside her, then reached to draw her into his arms. She snuggled close to him. For a while, they just sat, content to be with one another.

Finally, Dave spoke. "I'm so glad you're okay, Rylee." He felt her nod against his chest. "How did you know?"

She shrugged. "It was so bizarre, Dave, the box just sitting there against the back door. I didn't go close, but I knew it wasn't a regular delivery. We all know when and what day our deliveries come in." She leaned back to look up at him. "I just had a feeling something was wrong and went to warn everyone. Strangest thing is, not one person argued with me or hesitated to leave."

"People will be thinking you set it."

She stared at him, then nodded. "That's about what I would be expecting, now wouldn't it? I've talked to Frankie and Eddie.   They said there's not a lot of evidence right now, but teams will be searching when they can." Tears glistened for a moment in her eyes. "They also said they'd be putting out a statement."

Dave hugged her to him, noting that it was getting late. "So, other than that, how was your day?"

She started to laugh, relief sounding through it. "Only you, Dave, could face something like that, have me face it, then ask me how my day was. How was yours?"

"Very busy with the rain, but so much better now I'm with you." He stared into the distance.

She watched as he struggled to find the words and raised a hand to his cheek, feeling the roughness of the end-of-day stubble. "God was there, Dave. God protected all of us. I know you can't talk about what you did, but I just know God protected us both today."   His eyes had turned to her face as she spoke. "I think, after today, that I'm realizing just how short life can be, and that we'd be needing to seize every moment we can.   God is bringing healing to both of us. I can feel it inside me. I can see it in you, dear one."

Dave nodded, then reached to kiss her. Drawing back just a bit, he spoke, "So, Miss O'Shea, will you marry me this Saturday after all?"

She nodded, her lips meeting his again. "That I would be honoured to do, Mr. Allison.   Our plans haven't changed.   We hadn't told anyone that we were thinking of delaying anything."

Dave laid his head on hers. "I just wish we didn't have this thing hanging over our heads.   I know someone is still after you."

She sighed.   "I know, but maybe Frankie and Eddie will have it solved by then."

Dave laughed as he stood, reaching to pull her to her feet. "I highly doubt that will happen, sweetheart, but let's go tell your people the wedding is still on."

*****

Daniel and Miriam stared at each other as Dave walked away to leave, not surprised.

"I thought they were thinking of delaying it." Miriam spoke.

"What do you mean, dear?"

She shrugged. "Just a sense I had when I talked to Dave yesterday. Just a hesitation in his manner." She looked at her husband, standing leaning again the counter. "But I guess after today, they've decided not to."

Daniel walked over to hug his wife. "That would do it. I heard it was Rylee who warned everyone, taking a chance in going into all the buildings that were destroyed."

Miriam shuddered. "What a lady she is, Daniel. God surely protected her today." She looked up as Liana entered and dropped a bag on the table.

"What did I just miss? Dave passed me, practically walking on air."

"His wedding, Liana."

"I guessed that, but was there a problem? It's still on for Saturday, isn't it?"

Her parents nodded, then eyes narrowed watched her.

"Do you have an escort for Saturday, Liana?" Her father watched the emotions flickering across her face.

"I hadn't really thought about that, Dad, so no, I don't. I didn't think I'd need one. Now, tell me, do I?"

He shook his head. "No. I'm happy to escort my two ladies. Now, off to bed, everyone. It's been a long day."

Chapter 17

On Saturday, Abe stood at the back of the sanctuary, eyes alert. Dave had protested that he didn't need Abe's team there, but Abe had refused to back down. He knew better than Dave just how vulnerable the two would be on Saturday. His men were spread out throughout the whole area, eyes alert, weapons hidden beneath their suit coats. Dave had been there for them when they had needed him, even being kidnapped at one point to provide care for one of them, and they had no hesitation in being at his wedding. When Rylee had heard that Abe's men would be there, she had insisted their wives come as well. Ian's Lydia had made her peace with both Dave and Rylee over her attitude earlier.

Dave paced, his father watching him, a smile on his face. He remembered only too well how nervous he had been. He reached into his suit coat pocket and pulled out a package.

"Dave, I have something for you."

Dave turned, surprise on his face, as his father handed him the packet.

"Dad? Hair ties?"

Daniel smiled, a look of memory on his face. "Your mother used to wear her hair in a braid. I delighted in removing the ties and unbraiding it. I can see you're doing the same with Rylee. Give her those, tell her to put a supply in her pocket for over the day, and then you empty your pockets and return them to her at the end of the day. It's just a subtle way to flirt with your wife without others really knowing what's going on."

Dave stared at his father in shock, then began to laugh. "All these years, Dad, and you and Mom just carried on as if that was a normal thing to do. I can remember you doing that and Mom never getting mad at you, just sharing a look and a smile."

Daniel shook his head. "No, she never did." He looked up as Greg opened the office door. "It looks as if they're ready for us, son. Before we go out, Greg, I would like to pray once more with my son before he gets married."

Rylee was on the verge of tears, and nothing Fergus, Donovan, or Ailynne said to her helped. She was missing her parents so very badly that day, and nerves were making it worse. The three with her looked up as the door opened, and Mac and SuEllen stood there. Somehow, Mac had known how she would feel.

"Rylee." Mac had to say her name twice before she looked up, surprise on her face. "Rylee, you're a beautiful young lady. What part of Dave's heart you don't have now, you'll have by the time you get to him." He shared a look with SuEllen. "SuEllen faced something like you are. Her parents had died before we met. She was a basket case as we say here on our wedding day, missing her parents, just like you are." He pointed at Rylee, who nodded. "A dear lady in the church, wise beyond all measure, approached her that day. She told my sweetheart that her parents were with her in spirit, in thought and in memory, and more than likely they were standing right beside our dear Lord watching as she walked to meet me. The same is true for you, my dear. They're just not here in person, but they are with you."

Rylee struggled to control her tears, then reached to hug both Mac and SuEllen, clinging to SuEllen a bit more.

"I'd be thanking you both. That has helped." She tilted her head. "And who was this dear lady?"

The married couple exchanged a glance, knowing it would sadden Rylee when they told her. "It was Mrs. Caswell, dear." SuEllen looked at Rylee, seeing the surprise in her face. "Mrs. Caswell's husband was killed when they had only been married a few years. Their love stood the test of time. She told me she would never remarry. Only with them, it was his parents who were missing."

Ailynne drew her granddaughter close. "They're so right, my lass. Your parents are with you, in your heart, in your memories, and in all three of you. Now, no more tears. Dave's waiting for you, and your two brothers are getting restless. So, we have a wedding to get to. Let's go now."

They laughed at Ailynne's no nonsense voice and then followed her directions.

The three men wandered outside the church, far enough away that they couldn't be seen. They knew there was security there. They had seen them arrive, spend time in discussion, then move away. They had also seen the number of patrol cars making their way past or through the church parking lot. There would be no way to get to Rylee today. The leader finally moved away, leaving the two to watch. Somehow, they needed to get to her. Time was running out.

Dave turned as he sensed Rylee moving towards him, a hand on each brother's arm. He drew in his breath at her beauty, then reached for her hand, sharing a look with both Fergus and Donovan, who nodded.

Later that afternoon, Abe turned as his friend and business partner, Murphy, approached.

"We're all set when they are. Has Dave said where they're heading to?"

Abe shook his head. "He hasn't yet, but he said he would tell us when we set out. He left the impression they weren't going too far away."

Murphy nodded as his eyes, out of habit, scanned the area. "Joseph was watching a trio across the street. One man has left, but two are still there. Micah was able to snap some shots and send them on to Frankie."

"Do you really think they're out there?"

Murphy turned to Abe. "I do. It would be like them to try and snatch Rylee today, when neither one of them is thinking about security or safety." He sighed. "This is so different from what each of us went through. We were alert all the time, and things still happened to us. Dave doesn't have the same sense that we do. Sure, he was a medic in the armed forces, but he had people protecting him."

Abe nodded this time. "I know. I've tried to warn him, but it's not the same as being in the business." He looked up. "It seems they're ready to move."

*****

Rylee looked around the room Dave used as an office, then wandered over to the book shelves. He had added more for her books, and she was so thankful. She moved a couple of ornaments around, then turned once more. Dave, she knew, was on the phone in the kitchen, confirming his schedule. He was due back to work tomorrow and she would miss having him around all the time. She smiled as she remembered him handing her the packet of hair ties, telling her his father's words, and reached to feel for her braid. So far, she had replaced the ties at least six times already that day.

Dave stopped in the office doorway, watching as his wife stood there, lost in thought. All these years of waiting and praying, and he could finally say, his wife. He moved towards her and drew her to him.

"What are you thinking about so diligently, sweetheart?"

She shrugged. "Just being thankful, Dave, just being thankful."

He nodded, knowing what she meant. "I'm due in at 3 tomorrow afternoon. That means we'll be able to get to church in the morning."

She smiled. "That will be nice." She turned to face him, wrapping her arms around him. "Dave, I don't think we're done with these fellows yet. When we were away, I felt safe, knowing they weren't around. Coming home, I can feel the danger, feel like we are being watched."

Dave nodded. "I know what you mean. Abe has warned me, as have Frankie and Caleb. They're getting closer to the names and faces. Frankie said he'll have some photos soon for you and your brothers to look at."

Chapter 18

Parked in a coffee shop lot, Tom watched as Dave walked back towards him, coffees in his hand for them. It had been a quiet day so far for them, only a couple of runs. But he knew it could change in an instance.

"Here you go, Tom. It won't be as good as Gran makes, but it will have to do."

"You're comfortable with calling her that, aren't you, Dave?"

Dave nodded as he sipped the coffee, now lukewarm. "I am. I miss my own grandmothers, so she's filling in a spot in my heart. She's taken Liana in as well."

Tom nodded. "She does that. She just sweeps people into her heart."

Dave laughed. "That's a good way to put it. She does exactly that. She watches and weighs what's going on, then she just moves in on you."

"Any more word on those fellows after Rylee?"

Dave's face darkened. "No. Frankie's at a loss right now." Dave turned to Tom. "Micah caught pictures of them watching from across the street on our wedding day. If Abe's team hadn't been there, they likely would have snatched her."

"What!" Tom was shocked. "Are you serious?" At Dave's nod, he sat back, setting his coffee into the holder. "Wow! They really are serious, aren't they?"

"They are. Every moment I'm away from her, I worry."

"I can only imagine how much. I know how I would feel if it was my wife." Tom reached for the radio as tones sounded and listened to their call. "This sounds like a bad one, Dave."

"That it does." He reached for their work clipboard and started making notes, checking his watch for the time.

Dave sat for a moment, staring at the scene in front of him. "How did that happen?"

Tom shook his head. "I have no idea. Let's move."

The two men approached the accident in front of them, five vehicles in all, crushed, crumpled, tossed around by the speed of the collision. They went from vehicle to vehicle, assessing the patients, then turning as more help arrived.

An hour later, Dave walked beside the stretcher as they wheeled the last patient into the Emergency Room. Thankfully, there had been no deaths for them to deal with, but the injuries of some were severe. Dave knew that it was possible there would still be fatalities. This was one of those days it would be hard for him to wind down his day. *Lord, help me to leave this behind when I clock out. I don't want to take this home to Rylee.*

*****

Dave shut the door behind him and locked it. The lights were down low, he knew Rylee had left them that way for him. He searched through the house, disappointed not to find her up. Heading upstairs, he stopped, hearing a small noise from the kitchen. He retraced his steps and stopped in the doorway, a smile on his face. Rylee stood there. How had he missed her? Then he knew she had been out on the deck, in the dark, waiting for him to come home.

Rylee moved to hug her husband. She had been heading for bed when she had heard the news of the accident. She knew how hard it would be for him to set that aside and waited up for him.

"I'm so sorry, Dave."

He nodded, his cheek resting on her hair. "Thank you, lass. It's been a difficult few hours." He stopped, then continued. "Having you here to come home to has helped."

She drew back and took his hand, leading him back to the living room and sinking down on the couch. "This is when we need to pray, Dave, pray for healing for the victims, and healing for you."

Dave stopped, never having thought of it that way. He reached to cup her cheek, tears in his eyes. "How did I ever manage without your wisdom, Rylee? This is exactly what we need to do."

*****

Rylee turned from the counter, heading for the kitchen, when she heard her name called. Looking back, she saw both Eddie and Frankie heading her way. The few customers in the shop looked askance at them. Eddie nodded slightly at Rylee, then looked down into the display counter.

"What do you have that would be good for lunch today, Rylee? Peg wasn't feeling well today, so I told her I'd buy something."

Grateful for his consideration, Rylee nodded. "We have some pasties that are good."

He nodded. "That sounds good. I take two as well as some of your specialty cookies. Frankie, do you want the same?"

He nodded, his eyes searching the shop and then the street. "We'd be honoured if you'd join us for lunch, Rylee. It's not often we get to sit down with a master baker like you."

She blushed at his praise, then nodded at a table. "I'll bring them over to you as well as your coffee."

Eddie stopped her. "Tea for me, please, Rylee."

Rylee set their meals down and then seated herself. She waited for Eddie to ask the blessing.

"What were you wanting to talk to me about?" She went right to the point.

Eddie sighed, then took a bite of his pasty, savouring the mixture of meats. "These are good, Rylee. Let's eat. Then we'll talk."

She nodded, then looked across the room to where her grandmother stood, watching her.

Frankie wiped his mouth with his napkin, using that time to gather his thoughts on how to approach Rylee.

"Rylee, we have some photos we need you to look at. We can do it here, but we would rather you came to the department to do so." He watched her eyes, not seeing even a flicker of movement from them. "Some are connected to you parents. A couple of others, Micah snapped at your wedding."

She sighed. "Our wedding. They'd have been watching for us then, I gather you'd be saying?"

Eddie nodded. "That they were. Joseph said there had been three of them. Micah was only able to get pictures of two of them."

"And would Dave be knowing this?"

Frankie and Eddie exchanged a glance. "He just found out yesterday. With what happened on his shift, I would think he hadn't thought to tell you."

She shook her head, then gathered the debris from their lunch and stood. "Let me have a moment to let Gran know where I'd be heading. I'll be back."

Eddie stood outside the bake shop, eyes watching, turning as Rylee exited followed by Frankie.

Later that afternoon, Frankie walked beside her as she headed back for her shop.

"This isn't necessary, Frankie," she protested.

"We think it is, Rylee. Your confirmation on those photos as men you had seen with your father helps us. We know some of them were in the same organization as he was. It's those two that

Micah snapped photos of that we're concerned about."

She nodded, then glanced at Frankie. "But you can't be with me all the time, Frankie."

He sighed. "We know. Nor can Dave. We can only do so much. That's where we need you to be extra vigilant, Rylee, the way with the bomb. That bomb was meant to be left at your back door, you know."

Rylee stopped, horror in her face. "Ours? It's them?" When Frankie nodded, she raised her hands to her cheeks. "If Dave finds out, he'll never let me out of his sight until this is over."

"Rylee, he knows. He's the one who asked us about that."

She shuddered. "All those people could have been killed because of me?"

"No, not because of you. Because those men are after something you don't have."

She shook her head, eyes frightened. "I don't think I do, Frankie. I've given you everything I can think of that Da had. He didn't keep a lot, and his instructions were that when he died, we were to shred or burn all his work documents, which we did. So if there was something there, we don't have it any more. He didn't put anything to the computer, or save it that way. Not that we know of, anyway."

Frankie nodded. "That's what Fergus said. He remembers you and your grandmother going over everything and burning what would be his work records. Not that it would have likely helped."

"No, I don't remember much about them that would. It was more a matter of receipts than anything."

"Receipts?" Frankie held the door for her to the bake shop. "Do you remember anything about them? It might help."

She shook her head. "No, I don't. Gran might but she didn't read them either. We glanced at them, then burned them."

Rylee looked around, puzzled. Something wasn't right. Someone should have come from the back when she entered.

"Frankie, something's off. No one came from the back."

Frankie shot her a look, then reached for his weapon. "Stay right behind me, Rylee. I'm going through to the kitchen. Is there a cupboard or freezer they could have been locked into?

"Both."

Frankie said a prayer asking that the staff not be in the freezer, then headed for the kitchen, searching every corner of it, then heading for the back door. No sign that anything was wrong, other than no one where they should be.

A scrap of noise sounded behind him and he was down, blackness dropping quickly over him. He roused as he heard his name called. Eddie was bending over him.

"Frankie, can you sit up?" Eddie helped him to a sitting position. "What happened?"

Frankie groaned as his head pounded with pain. "There wasn't anyone in the kitchen when we got back here. I was looking around and got clobbered. Do you see my gun?"

Eddie handed it to him. "We found Ailynne and the two staff locked into the cupboard, but no sign of Rylee."

Frankie's eyes slid closed. "How did I let that happen, Eddie? I told her to stay with me, right behind me as I searched."

"They were waiting for you, Frankie, and ambushed you." Eddie stood, his eyes searching the area. "I don't see a lot of evidence but our team's on their way."

"How'd you come to be here?"

Eddie shrugged. "When you didn't get back, I came looking for you. It's only been about ten or fifteen minutes."

"So where did they take her? It had to be out the back door. And I didn't see a vehicle out there waiting."

"Now that's strange." Eddie turned to a patrol office. "Start by searching the buildings on either side. Have someone go through what remains of the demolished buildings."

*****

Ken faced Dave across the bench in their change room, Tom standing close behind Dave.

"Eddie called, Dave."

Dave's face whitened as his fingers gripped his jacket tighter. This couldn't be good. "Rylee?"

Ken nodded. "Eddie and Frankie had her look at some pictures today. Then Frankie walked her back to the bake shop. She noticed no one was there, and Frankie went to check it out. He had Rylee with him as he did so." Ken stopped, and Dave knew what was coming.

"They got her, didn't they, Ken?"

Ken nodded. "That's what they're surmising. They took Frankie down and Rylee disappeared."

"I need to get there." Dave moved to pass Ken but stopped when Ken put his hand out to stop him.

"Eddie's sent one of the detectives, Jake Wilson, to get you. They don't want you on your own right now."

Dave shoved past Ken. "It doesn't matter about me. I want to find my wife."

"It does matter, Dave." Tom's voice stopped him. "If she won't tell them what they want, you'll be taken to put the pressure on her. Don't you see that? It was just a matter of which one they could get to first."

Dave's eyes slid closed. "You're right, Tom. We talked about that, Rylee and I, just last night." He opened his eyes, finding Jake watching him. "Jake, let's go."

Tom and Ken watched him walk away. Tom finally spoke.

"Match me up with someone for the next few shifts, Ken. Dave's not going to be up to working."

"Already have, Tom. Go after him. He'll need to know we support him."

"He does, Ken. Just pray Rylee's still alive and they can find her."

Chapter 19

Setting the carafe back on the burner after pouring a cup of coffee, what number it was he had lost track of, Dave stared out the window with burning, tear-filled eyes. Lord, where is she?   I know You're in control, but where is Rylee? Is she safe and unharmed?

Dave turned as he heard a throat cleared behind him.   Frankie stood there, flanked by Abe and Emma.

"Dave.   Come sit with us for a few minutes." Frankie's eyes studied his friend, and his heart sank. He was going through so much.

Dave finally nodded, fatigue weighing him down.   He moved slowly to the table and sat, the others finding chairs around it.

"What news do you have, Frankie?"

Frankie shook his head.   "Not a lot. We did get some security video, and our team's cleaning it up to try and find Rylee and her abductors."

"So, there hasn't been a lot of movement is what you're saying?"

"No, I'm not.   We've found fingerprints and they're being run. Some have already come back as the men in the photos. Teams are out right now tracking them down." He looked at Abe and Emma. "Emma and Jace are working their magic again, Dave. They've found information on these men that we didn't have: aliases, government documents, travel documents. All this is helping us narrow down where they are. They're still in town, somewhere."

"And right now, Rylee is with them, somewhere. How do we know if she's even still alive?" Dave swiped at his eyes to clear them.

Frankie nodded, then looked at Abe.

"Dave, our team's working on this as well. Micah's researching everything he can get his hands on. Gideon's pulled himself in as well as Sidney. We'll find her."

Dave shoved back from the table and went to stand, staring out the back door, leaving the three to exchange glances, then watch him. Frankie excused himself as a call came in he had to take.

"Dave." Emma's voice was soft, but still caused him to turn around to face her. "Abe and I know how difficult this is for you. We didn't face this exactly, but you know what we went through. You know what Abe's guys went through. Let us help you."

He finally nodded and returned to his seat. "How?"

"How?" Abe shared a look with Emma. "For now, we have someone with you all the time. Ken's found someone to cover your next few shifts. Micah will work his magic. Joseph's monitoring your security system."

Dave nodded, knowing that his friends were looking out for him. He looked up as Greg appeared in the doorway. He knew his father was somewhere around the house as were Fergus and Donovan.

"Greg. Let me get you a coffee."

"I've got it, Dave." Greg poured his coffee, then sat where Frankie had been, just watching his friend.

"What? No platitudes, Greg? No she's fine? No God's got her?" Dave was hitting out, the pain increasing with each moment Rylee was missing.

Greg shook his head. "None of those, Dave. You know me better than that. We've both served overseas, so we know those kinds of platitudes are just words. It's what we believe in our heart that matters."

Dave stared at his friend, uncertain as to what he was saying that. "What do you mean?"

"Just what I said. What does your heart say about Rylee?"

Dave sank back in his chair, eyes on the mug he was twisting in his hands. He realized then that he had deliberately chosen Rylee's favourite mug. "You're right, Greg. It's what in my heart." He pointed to the mug. "This is Rylee's. Taking it made me feel closer to her." He straightened up again, determination crossing his face. "Abe, how do we find her? I know Frankie's got people looking but we need to think differently than they do."

Emma spoke up. "You're exactly right, Dave." She looked around. "Do you have paper and pen?"

He started to rise. "In the office." Abe motioned him back down and then returned with a pad and pen for his wife.

"What are you thinking, Emma?"

She held up a finger as she rapidly penned words on the pad. "Dave, Greg. Help me out. If this had been overseas, what kinds of areas would she be hidden in? Buildings? Caves? Boats?"

Frankie listened from the hallway, his phone still to his ear as he waited for Eddie to come back on the line. He nodded. Emma was good at what she did. It would be a race between the two of them to see who found Rylee first, and he wasn't sure his teams would be the one. His attention was caught by what Eddie was relaying to him. He turned, searching for Daniel and finding him.

Frankie pulled his phone out again as it chimed. If this kept up, he thought, I'll be heading back to office to recharge it.

"What do you have, Doug?"

Doug spoke rapidly, his tone calm but forceful. Frankie shot a look behind him at

Dave, then searched for Eddie, heading towards him.

"Eddie, got a moment?" he asked as he pocketed his phone.

Eddie turned, then walked with him outside. "What do you have, Frankie?"

"Doug's team has found the vehicle we were looking for, out by the quarry. I'm sending out search teams that way."

"But you don't think she's there."

Frankie shook his head. "Would you?"

"No, I wouldn't," Eddie agreed. "It's likely something to throw us off." He watched as Micah rushed past them. "Now, what's he up to?"

Frankie turned to watch. "For Micah to be running like that, it's something big. Listen, I'm heading back for the office. I want to see what the teams are coming up with."

"I'm going to hang around here for a while." Eddie watched as Michael appeared. "Now, why is Michael here?"

Michael nodded at Eddie, then stopped. "Any word yet, Eddie?"

Eddie shook his head.

Frankie studied him, then asked, "And why would you be asking, Michael? Aren't you just home visiting family?"

Michael looked around, then spoke. "I'm here, not just for that. I worked with the organization that Rylee's father did. They've always had suspicions about his death. Recent scuttlebutt we've heard said it was murder, and they sent me here."

"And no one bothered to talk to us?" Frankie was angry.

"Calm down, Frankie. We don't need your anger at this point. We had no proof, and you wouldn't have believed us, now would you?"

Eddie had to agree. "So what proof do you have?"

"Photos, voice logs, voice mail, emails, tapes, legal documents." Michael stopped for a moment. "It's all in a box at the bank right now. I was ready to turn it all over to you tomorrow, but they've pre-empted that."

"Do you know who they are?"

Michael nodded. "I do. They're very nasty people. We can track them to multiple murders. Her parents are just a pebble in the rock pile they created. I can give you names and photos tonight but not where they are staying. They packed up from the house they were using."

"And where was that?"

Michael pointed across the street. "That one. They've been this close to Dave and Rylee. I just found that out about an hour ago."

"This close?" Eddie's voice rose, then fell. "This close all the time?"

Michael nodded once again. "Listen, I need to slip away. I can't let them know I was talking with you about this."

"I think it's too late for that, Michael." Eddie watched as Ian and Murphy flanked Michael. "These two men are from Abe's security team. I want you to go with them for tonight."

Michael sighed. "I guess I can, but make sure you watch Dave. If Rylee doesn't speak, they'll nab him to make her."

"She doesn't know anything, Michael. We've talked with her. She has nothing left that was her father's now, other than a few mementos and photos."

Michael searched Eddie's face. "Then that's it then, isn't it? Pray they release her."

Ian and Murphy shared a look with Eddie, Murphy nodding, before they walked away with Michael. Eddie sighed, knowing how close to the wire it was coming. *Lord, we need a miracle, please. Help us find her.*

Chapter 20

The man stood, watching as Michael was led away. He couldn't put a name to him, but he knew he was bad news for their group. He didn't dare check his phone, lest the light give him away. It had been vibrating off and on for the couple of hours he had been standing there watching. His eyes turned to the house. They would have no chance of grabbing Dave, he was too closely watched. The same for her grandmother and her brothers. In fact, they couldn't find her grandmother right now.

He watched as some of the patrol cars left, just one or two remaining as well as an unmarked cruiser. Other vehicles remained as well. Dave was too well guarded, the man thought once again, then stopped as he felt metal at his ear.

Jake Wilson had seen movement from the yard across the street, in the yard of a supposedly vacant home. He had motioned for a couple of men to follow me, Joseph trailing along with them. Joseph had spotted the man and crept on silent feet towards him, his weapon at the ready.

"I'll take that, if you don't mind." Joseph reached for the weapon that man had drawn. "Jake, over here."

"Good work, Joseph. Here, let me take that." He reached for the weapon and secured it, then dropped it into an evidence bag. "Read him his rights, guys, then head downtown with him."

Joseph and Jake watched him walk away, defiant even under arrest.

"He won't talk, you know." Joseph turned to walk back across the street.

"Not likely, but I think he's one of the bombers. He looks like the photo we were able to pull."

Joseph stopped, then continued to walk. "Good luck with that. He'll lawyer up."

"But if we can tie him to the bombing, we'll have his bail set high."

"I don't think that's a concern of his. He'll make it."

"Then pray we find Rylee in the next twenty-four hours."

*****

Dave looked up as Micah beckoned for Abe.   Abe excused himself and then stood at the kitchen doorway talking with Micah. He finally turned to watch Dave.

"Dave, Micah has a good idea where Rylee is, but we need to confirm that."

"How?"   Dave rose to his feet, catching his balance with his hand on his chair.

"Micah figured something like this would happen. Those earrings Rylee's been wearing.   Micah now tells me they have a GPS tracker in them."

"What?" Dave was shocked.

"Hold on, Dave.   It's what I set up with Luke's wife. They are only activated if the woman activates them.   That's how we tracked Abi.   It looks as if Rylee's finally been able to activate hers."

"And just when did you plan to tell me this?"

Micah shook his head. "Rylee promised me she'd tell you yesterday. I gave them to her before your wedding."

Dave sank back on his chair and rubbed his hands up and down his face. "We didn't have much of a chance to talk last night. She was more concerned about that accident I had to respond to."

Abe and Micah exchanged glances. That's about what they had figured, that Rylee hadn't had a chance to speak with Dave.

"Where is she, Micah?" Dave looked up at him.

"She seems to be in a building near the edge of town. Caleb was sending Doug and his team there to see if they could find her." Micah hesitated. "We have paramedics standing by as well."

"I want to be there."

Abe shoved Dave back into his chair. "Once we have confirmation, we'll get you there. Right now, we're trying to keep as much vehicle traffic away from there as we can."

Dave stared at Abe, refusing to back down. "Take me there, Abe, right now."

Abe shook his head. "Not happening, Dave. Joseph just told me Jake's arrested a man who was standing across the street from here, likely waiting until you were on your own. Then he would have moved in."

Dave sat back, shock on his face. "Across the street?"

Abe nodded, catching Emma's eyes, then frowning at her. "Emma, what do you have?"

Emma stared at Abe as she spoke. "Jace just sent me word. The ones who did the bombing? They're all part of the group Rylee's father was after." A movement at the doorway caught her attention. Fergus and Donovan stood there. "We're closing in on them, guys."

"Not quickly enough, it seems." Fergus spat out the words, then turned and walked away.

Donovan shrugged his shoulders, an apologetic look on his face, before he headed after his brother.

Abe watched as Micah ran from the house, Joseph on his heels. Something was moving, he thought.

Emma continued to talk in a quiet manner with Dave, and Abe could see Dave calming down. Walking through the house, he found Daniel, seated in the office, head bowed in prayer. Stepping backwards, he walked away, pulling out his phone as it vibrated.

"Abe. Micah. Doug's been through the house. It's still showing that Rylee's there somewhere, but he can't find her."

"I'm on my way. What house is it? The old Miller place? They have a crawl space, if I remember rightly. There's a trap door somewhere in the kitchen or pantry. Tell Doug that. I'll be there in fifteen."

He motioned for Luke to go with him, stopped for a quick word with Matt, then headed for his vehicle, sending a quick text to Emma.

"Where'd Abe go, Emma?" Dave hadn't missed the face that Abe left.

She sighed. "You know Abe too well, Dave. Micah asked him to go check something for him."

"They've found Rylee, haven't they?"

"Not that I know of, Dave. Abe would have told you that before he left."

"Not if she was dead, he wouldn't. Not until he had seen her himself."

Emma nodded. "You're right on that. So we can only speculate that she's still alive. Pray, Dave. That's what you can do. Pray for your wife."

Dave rose, leaving the kitchen, his thoughts in turmoil. How do I pray, Lord, what do I say? Daniel watched as Dave stood in the office, staring out into the daylight. He knew there wasn't anything he could do but pray.

*****

Abe pulled to a halt near Joseph's vehicle and slid from behind the wheel. "Micah, what do you have?"

"It's still showing her as being here, Abe. Doug can't find the trap door. There's new flooring down, he says in those two rooms."

Abe nodded and then ran for the house. He had a good idea of where the trap door was.

"Doug, where have you searched?"

"All over the kitchen and pantry. There's new flooring down, Abe. It looks like it was just put down."

"Find me a pry bar, if you can, or something to start pulling up the flooring." He looked around. "This place is falling apart. Why put down new flooring?"

Doug stopped on his way to find a bar. "That's what has me puzzled. Do you really think she's down there?"

Abe nodded. "I think so. I suspect she couldn't or wouldn't tell them anything, so they decided to get rid of her. Just pray we're in time."

Abe stomped on the floor, listening intently for the subtle sounds coming back at him. His eyes searched the area.

Hearing yells and shouts from outside the house, he stopped, then continued hunting. Tired of waiting for Doug to come back, he reached for the baseboard and working his fingers behind it, began pulling at it. Throwing it aside, he began pulling at the flooring, flinging the boards away from him.

Doug appeared with a pry bar, looked at Abe and then at the bar. "Guess you don't need this."

Abe reached for it. "It will make the task go quicker. You throw as I pull the boards. If I can remember, I should be near where the trap door is." He shot a quick look at Doug. "What was going on outside?"

"They caught a couple of fellows watching the place. Patrol is taking them in."

Finally, Abe could see the framework for the door and pulled even harder and faster. He looked up as Luke appeared at the door with Doug's second-in-command.

"Find the paramedics, Luke. We'll be through shortly. If she's down there, we'll need them."

Abe shoved the bar into the space around the trap door and pried, Doug grabbing for it as it raised, throwing it back onto the pile of flooring.

"I need a light!" Doug's voice echoed through the house. Grabbing the one handed him, he shone it down into the crawl space. "We've got trouble, Abe. There's at least six inches of water down there."

Abe shot him a look, then dropped through the hole, water splashing around him as he landed. "Hand me the light." He shone it around as Doug dropped down beside him. Crouching, the men searched desperately for Rylee.

"I've got her, Abe." Doug's voice rang with triumph. "She's alive, thank God."

Abe shone the light towards Doug's voice, catching him as he gathered Rylee into his arms, and then made his way back towards the trap door. He handed her through to Luke, then pulled himself through, reaching back for the flashlight, then giving Abe a hand back up.

Luke ran for the paramedics, praying that she would survive. He could feel the cold chill and wet that soaked through his jacket. How long had she been down there? Long enough he knew for them to have replaced the flooring and baseboards. That wasn't the work of just a few minutes.

Chapter 21

Dave looked up as his father shook his shoulder.   It had been twenty-four hours since Rylee had disappeared. He rubbed his blurry eyes and sat up

"Dave." Daniel waited. "Dave. Look at me."

Dave finally raised his head enough he could see his father. "What?"

"Dave. Abe and Doug found Rylee. She's at the hospital right now. Come, let's get you there."

Dave sat, staring at his father. "Rylee? They found her?"   His father nodded. "She's alive."

"She is, Dave, but she's in trouble. We need to get you to her." He reached to steady his son as he stood on shaky legs, his hand on Dave's arm as he walked through the house.

Eddie was waiting for them and tucked Dave into the back of his car. Daniel watched from the front seat as Dave sank back, trying to gather his thoughts and prepare himself for what he would find.

"What did they say, Dad?"

"Abe didn't say much other than that they found her in the crawl space at the old Miller place."

"The crawl space?" Dave's voice rose a fraction of a tone. "That place is practically falling apart." He stopped, his eyes meeting his father's. "They found her in water, didn't they? Freezing cold water?"

Daniel sighed, then nodded. "They did, Dave. But they had paramedics right there, waiting, Abe said Paul and Carol. Ken was there too."

Dave nodded, knowing Ken had sent the best he had to help. Lord, please. Keep her alive. I can't lose her yet.

Dave waited impatiently as Eddie pulled the back door open for him, then was out and through the Emergency doors, heading for the registration desk.

The clerk looked up, recognizing Dave.

"Dave. What brings you here?"

"My wife."

The clerk sat stunned, staring at him. She hadn't heard that Dave had married.

"Betty, Rylee Allison was just brought in. Where is she?"

Betty finally got the connection. "Dr. Thompson's with her now. Let me go tell him." She shook her head as he started to head back. "Not this time, Dave. This time, you need to wait, please."

Dave stopped, frustrated at having to wait. Daniel turned him back to the waiting room.

"Come, Dave. We'll wait here. You can see when they come for you from here."

Dave nodded as he sank down into a chair. He was exhausted, far beyond anything he had felt in years. His heart was raised in prayer as he waited, not seeing the men and women moving around him, his eyes focused solely on the door to where he knew his wife lay.

Dr. John Thompson, Emergency physician and friend of many from his church, looked up as Betty tapped at the door, then peeked in.

"Dave's here, Dr. Thompson."

"Dave?"

"Dave Allison. Rylee's his wife."

John stopped for a moment. "They've kept that secret well. I didn't know." He turned back to Rylee, listening to her heart and lungs. "We need to hook her up to the heart monitor, Sue. Then we'll need some X-Rays. I don't like the sound of her breathing. You've pulled blood?"

"I have and sent it already. The lab said they'd rush it for you." Sue reached for another IV. "Do you think they drugged her?"

John shook his head. "I don't think they did, but we need to ensure that. We also need to work on warming her up. She's chilled through and through."

"Hypothermia?"

John nodded. "I think so. Does anyone know how long she was in the water?"

Carol spoke from the corner she had tucked herself into while Paul restocked their rig. "They don't know, but it was long enough for the men who kidnapped her to re-lay a floor in a small kitchen."

John spun to stare at her. "What did you just say?"

"Doug and Abe found her in the crawl space at the old Miller place. I don't know how, they didn't say. But Abe had to pull up the floor in the kitchen to find the trap door."

John stared at her for a moment, then turned back to Rylee, working and praying at the same time. "Did they catch the men?"

Carol shook her head, then realizing he had his back to her, spoke. "I haven't heard, but they weren't at that home while we were there."

John drew a deep breath. "They left her to die then, figuring no one would find her for years." He glanced up at Sue, catching the look on her face. "Have them bring the portable X-Ray in, Sue. I don't want to move her from here. Make sure to keep the heated blankets on her."

He turned as the lab tech returned, handing him some of the blood work. "So far, no sign of any drugs." He turned to study Rylee's face. "They worked her over well, though, didn't they? She mustn't have told them what they wanted. It wasn't about money, do you know?"

Sue shook her head. "Frankie didn't say."

John nodded, standing back to watch the monitors. "I don't like that heart rhythm, Sue. Can you reach Stephen? I think he's on call today."

"He is and he's here, up in ICU. I'll call there for him."

"Thank you." He stood watching for a few minutes, then turned as Carol moved towards the door. "Thank you, Carol. You two did a good job stabilizing her and getting her here. I suspect Dave's waiting out there. Don't stop and talk with him. If he stops you, tell him I'll be coming out for him in a minute or two."

Carol nodded, knowing that Dave would be watching for them.

Dave looked up as Carol and Paul walked towards him, then stood.

"She's in good hands, Dave. John's working with her. He'll be out shortly to speak with you."

"Thank you, both of you." Dave's voice died away. The two nodded and moved away.

Dave paced, waiting for what, he wasn't sure. He knew he had friends waiting, and looked up as Fergus, Donovan and Ailynne came towards him.

"Any word yet, Dave?" Fergus' voice was tight.

"Not yet. John Thompson is to come out shortly. Come, Ailynne, sit by Dad."

Dave turned as his father touched his shoulder. "Caleb's here, Dave. He would like a word with you."

Dave nodded, excused himself to head towards Caleb, then changed his course when he saw John heading his way.

John drew Dave back into the unit. "It's different this time for you, Dave."

Dave nodded, his eyes on John. "How is she, John?"

John sighed, watching his young friend, knowing Dave would take nothing less than the truth, seeing the signs of the stress and strain lining his face and weighing down his body. "She's alive right now,

Dave. I have no idea how long she was in that crawl space or in the water. I'm told it took Abe and Doug pulling up a floor to get to her." He stopped as he looked at Dave's face. "They hadn't told you all of it yet, have they?"

Dave shook his head, then looked back behind him. "That's likely what Caleb was looking to tell me. Continue, John."

"We're treating her for hypothermia, checking for pneumonia. That's part of what I think she has. She was beaten as well, Dave. She has a lot of bruising on the face and around the abdominal area. There's also another issue we need to address." He reached to pull Dave aside as a stretcher was wheeled past them. "Her heart rhythm seems to be affected in some way. I've called in Stephen Black. He's with her now, making his assessment."

Dave's eyes sought the room where Rylee was laying. "Her heart?"

John nodded. "It's something we needed to check out, Dave. We'll see what Stephen has to say." He pointed at the door. "Come on. Let's get you to her."

Dave paused before he entered, his heart raised in prayer. He stopped inside the door, watching as Sue worked around Rylee, and a physician he didn't know bending over her, stethoscope to her chest.

He stopped once again as he stood near her bedside, eyes tracing her face. He winced as he saw the bruising. What did they do, Lord? How could they beat her and then leave her like that?

He heard the two physicians talking and moved closer to Rylee, reaching to touch her face. Her hands were tucked under a blanket he realized would be heated, trying to warm her body.

He looked up as he heard John say his name.

"Dave, I think you've met Stephen Black in passing. He's the cardiologist I spoke with you about."

Dave nodded, his eyes focused on the physician's face. "How is she?"

Stephen shared a look with John, then looked back at Dave. "So far, it's okay. You know that with hypothermia, the heart rhythm can be affected. That's what happened here. Doug did say the water was not real icy, but was cold. Somehow, she managed to find somewhere she could get out of the water to some extent. That helped."

Dave nodded. "So now what?"

"Right now, we're working to stabilize her. Then we'll send her up to critical care where we can monitor her heart better. There's a chance she has pneumonia, but John's already started the treatment for that."

Dave nodded, trying to absorb what he already knew from his work, and how it applied to the one he loved. "I want to stay with her, John."

"You can for the most part, Dave, but there will be times you'll need to leave. Are her brothers and grandmother out there?"

He sighed, knowing he needed to go talk with them. He turned, as he spoke, "They are. So are my people."

John stopped him and caught him as he staggered, pushing him down into a chair. "Stay here, Dave. I'll go get them. They can come in for a bit, until we need to move her."

Ailynne approached Dave, wrapping her arm around him as she reached to touch Rylee. "John spoke with us, Dave, and told us what we're facing. God is there." She looked up at her grandsons. "Anger is fine, but don't direct it at God."

They nodded, having had this conversation with her in the past. "We know, Gran. It's just angers us that they haven't found them yet."

"They will. There are too many people looking for them."

Dave stepped away. He needed a chance to recover his emotions. He looked up to see his parents watching him, Liana standing beside their mom. Miriam reached to hug her son, bringing his tears to the surface. Daniel's arms went around all three of his family as he prayed.

"What are they saying, Dave?" Liana was finally able to speak.

"Hypothermia, pneumonia, abnormal heart rhythm." He paused, his eyes meeting his father's. "She was beaten, Dad, beaten and then dropped into water in a crawl space, and a floor replaced over it. What kind of monster does that?" He heard the quick intake of his mother's breath.

"I don't know, Dave. Eddie's coming back in a bit. He headed to the department to find out where the investigation stands."

"I can tell you where it stands. Just where it stood yesterday at this time. They haven't found the men. They say they're looking, but where are those monsters?"

Dave pulled himself out of the chair he had been perched in all night, scrubbing his hands down his face. He needed a shower and a shave but there was no way he was leaving Rylee. She was still unconscious, but the nurse said her core body temperature was back to almost normal. They had dodged the pneumonia, thankfully, he thought. Now, to hear that the heart rhythm was back to normal. He studied the monitors, not liking what he saw on the heart monitor. He prayed there was no lasting damage.

He turned as the door to the room opened. Frankie stood for a minute, holding open the door, before he entered, the door swishing closed silently behind him. He listened to the beeps of the monitors, then turned to Dave.

"How is she this morning, Dave?"

Dave shrugged. "Temperature's about normal and there's no pneumonia. Her beating didn't damage any internal organs, but they're concerned that she hasn't made a move to awaken yet. They're talking about doing a CT of the brain. Her heart's still not right either."

"Greg has the prayer line working around the clock for you two." He paused, struggling to find the words he needed to. "Listen, I wanted to update you on the case."

"Have you found the monsters yet?"

"Not yet, but we're closing in. People are reporting sightings of them, Dave, people who value what you have done for them and the community." Dave's eyes never left his face. "I don't think you understand your value in the community. Our officers are being stopped all the time right now, with people giving information and asking how the two of you are."

Dave slowly nodded. "But that doesn't answer the question. Where are they?"

"Not in the hospital. We have that closed down tight. Abe's men are here. So is Don Woods' security team. Off duty officers are all around as well. They can't get to her. We're checking IDs. John and

Stephen have restricted which nurses are hers."

Dave nodded again. "Sounds like you have the protective duty there. But it still doesn't sound like you've found them."

"We will, Dave. We will. Emma and Jace are working non-stop, feeding us information as soon as they find it."

Frankie turned as a tap came to the door, and Jake peeked in, motioning him outside.

"Listen, Dave, I have to run. I'll be back in a while."

Dave gave a curt nod, his eyes once more on Rylee as she stirred slightly. He pulled his chair closer and reached for her hand. Thank you, Lord, she's still here. Heal her, please.

Hours later, Daniel found Dave in the same position and hesitated before he spoke.

"Dave, have you eaten today?"

Dave roused, then shook his head. "No, I haven't, Dad. I haven't wanted to leave Rylee."

"I didn't think you had. Here's some soup and a sandwich your Mom made for you. Eat. You'll need your strength."

Dave nodded as he reached for the food his father had brought for him. "Frankie was around earlier. They haven't found them yet."

"Yes, I think they have. I met Frankie down stairs. He seems to think they've found them all."

Dave's eyes slid shut. "I pray they do. Talk to Michael, will you, Dad? He never said anything to you, but he's involved in some way. Make sure that they have everyone. I can't go through this again."

Standing just inside the door, Frankie looked back as the door cracked open. Michael stood there, a puzzled look on his face. Frankie headed towards him as Michael backed away.

"It's time we had a talk, Michael. No more throwing up blinds and leading us down the wrong path. Dave says you're involved, and I tend to believe him."

Michael nodded and then sighed. "That I am, Frankie, but not how you think. I'm not one of the bad guys in this."

"Then tell me who you really are."

Michael looked around, then pulled out his wallet, extracting a single card from it. "This is who I am, Frankie. I was sworn to secrecy when I came. I did know Rylee's father and worked with him for a few months. Then I was pulled into a different investigation, one involving human trafficking for labour. Rylee's Dad worked in the area of stolen treasures."

Frankie listened at Michael talked, taking notes as fast as he could. "Why didn't you just come to us in the first place?"

Michael shook his head. "I couldn't. I wasn't even sure if I was on the right track with this. Rylee's Dad happened onto something in his investigation, and we don't know what it is. I don't think we will ever know."

Frankie nodded. "I suspect you're right. Now, this is what we're going to do. Jake is standing right behind you, and he's taking you to the department and taking your statement." He looked behind him at the door he had closed. "I need to speak with Dave."

"That's not a good idea." Michael went to stop him.

"No, you're not calling the shots here any more, Michael. I'll place you under arrest as an accomplice if I have to." Jake nodded as he caught Frankie's eye. "Jake will too. Now off with you. Don't try anything, you hear me?"

Dave stood in the doorway, watching as Frankie turned. "Did he finally talk to you, Frankie?"

"You knew about this but didn't say anything? You might have prevented what happened to your wife." Frankie was plainly angry with Dave as he pointed towards Rylee.

"Back off, Frankie. At the time, I made the decision to support a friend when he asked. He was to go and talk with Eddie. He made that promise to me. Whether he did or not, you'll need to talk to Eddie. We have no way of knowing if this could have been prevented. My gut says no." With that, Dave shut the door in Frankie's face and paced back to his chair beside Rylee.

The man sitting in the waiting room watched all that was going on. He wasn't close enough to hear but he nodded to himself. Something had happened. He needed to take advantage of the split in the friends while he could, but he couldn't get near the door for security people. Somehow he had to manage it. His people had been arrested. He was convinced Rylee still knew something. Then he turned and walked away. He would try her brothers and her grandmother first. They might be easier to get to.

*****

Donovan looked up as the man approached him, gave a half smile, then went to walk by him. He stopped as he saw the weapon in the man's hand.

"We're heading back to your home, boy. Now, turn around. Is your brother there?"

Donovan shook his head. "He's not. What's this about?" He felt the weapon poke into his side.

"No questions from you. I'll do the asking."

Donovan keyed in the security password as he was directed to and then closed the door, spinning to face the man.

"What is it you want?"

"You know exactly what I want."

Donovan shook his head. "No, I don't. I have no idea what it is."

"Your father had information on us. I want that."

Donovan stared at him. "We have no information on anyone. Anything Rylee found she turned over to the police. What makes you think we have more?" Donovan's head flew to the side at the brutal strike across his face. His hand went up to touch the side of his mouth, tasting the blood from his split lip.

"There has to be something here. She can't have turned it all in. To your office, boy, and no tricks."

Donovan nodded, then regretted it. He turned for the office, vainly trying to come up with a plan. He didn't know the man, but he had no doubt he would shoot him in cold blood if he didn't find what he wanted. He knew his phone's volume was turned down, and he reached into his pocket, frantically pressing 911 to call for help.

"Where do you want me to start looking?" Donovan asked, spinning to face the man once more.

The man's eyes flew around the room. "Where are his records?"

"We don't have them. We burnt them."

"I don't mean paper records. He had a system that didn't involve paper. He had certain objects that kept track of what he had found. Where are they?"

Donovan again shook his head. "Da never spoke about anything like that, so how would I know?"

The man advanced, weapon raised and pointing at Donovan's head. "You do know. I heard your father say you did. He called it a game or something like that."

Donovan's mind was racing. So that's what that was, he thought. It really wasn't a game after all. He kept his thoughts off his face as he shrugged. "We don't have anything like that for you. We didn't keep anything much from when our parents were alive."

A sound at the door caught the man's attention. Taking advantage of that split second, Donovan lunged at him, falling short of his object, and landing with a thud on the floor as the man's weapon descended on him. The man searched the office, tossing books and ornaments from his way. It wasn't there. Where was it? Had she taken it with her? He knew he would never get into Dave's house without help. His sister - yes, he would find Dave's sister and use her.

*****

Fergus dropped to his knees beside his brother, reaching out a shaking hand to find a pulse. Calling for his grandmother, he punched in the numbers to call for help.

Ailynne stood once more in the Emergency Department waiting to hear about a grandchild. Fergus kept his arm around her. Eddie found them, as did Abe.

"What happened, Fergus?"

Fergus shook his head. "I don't know. We came in and found him unconscious in the office. It had been tossed. The security system was turned off, so it had to have been Donovan that did it. Somehow he called 911. When I called, I was told officers were responding. So how did this happen?"

Abe stood and listened, then spoke, coming up with a plan to keep the three of them safe. Ailynne objected, stating she needed to be at the bake shop.

Abe laughed, stating Ian would be with her. "Ian loves to cook and bake. He'll be in his glory with you, Ailynne."

Eddie drew Abe away from them. "We need to talk to Dave, Abe. This is now going further than we thought."

Abe nodded as he watched Fergus and his grandmother taken back to Donovan. "If you'll talk to Donovan, I'll head upstairs."

Abe stood for a moment outside Rylee's door. Nathaniel looked at him, looked around, then brought his eyes back to Abe.

"What happened, Abe? I can tell something did."

"It did.   Donovan was knocked unconscious at their home, and the office was tossed.   Someone was looking for something and didn't find it, I would suspect. We're not done here, not by a long shot."

Nathaniel nodded, looking past Abe. "Don Woods is here as well as Gideon and Sidney.   Who do you want to go with Rylee's family?"

"Pick a couple and send them with them.   Donovan's still downstairs, so we should have someone there.   Try some of Don's men. I know you guys won't want to leave Dave.   I told Ailynne Ian would be with her at the shop."

"You've got that right. Dave's been in and out for the last little bit. He says Rylee's waking up more and more all the time."

"That's good news. Any word on her heart?"

Nathaniel stared at Abe. "Her heart? Was there an issue?"

Abe sighed.   "Dave didn't tell you? The physicians are concerned as there were some irregular rhythms to it after she was brought in. That's why she on this floor."

"We all wondered but we didn't want to ask." Nathaniel looked behind him at the door. "No wonder Dave looks like he does."

"That would do it. Don's heading our way. Talk to him for me, will you? I'll be back out in a while."

Dave looked up as Abe entered, then turned his eyes back to Rylee. He had been assured that she was sleeping naturally now, but he still watched the heart monitor, willing her heart rhythm to return to normal. The physicians had assured him it was improving but they still needed to monitor her.

"Dave, can we talk for a minute?" Abe watched as his friend turned back to him. "Have you gotten any sleep at all?"

Dave nodded. "Some in bits and pieces. What do you need?"

Abe paused, then spoke. "Donovan was attacked tonight in their home. It looks, from what Eddie says, that the man was let into the house or made Donovan take him in. He tossed the office, looking for something. Eddie hasn't been able to talk with Donovan yet."

"We're still not done?" Dave was frustrated. "I thought they had arrested all of them."

"Apparently not the boss. That means we don't pull our security off you. Don Woods is heading down to watch for Rylee's folks. What about your people?"

"They should be safe. Just watch Liana. After being overseas, she's not as careful here as she should be."

Abe nodded. "How be we take her out to our place? Emma will watch her for you."

"That would work. Do it tonight please."

Abe pulled out his phone and sent a text. "Gideon and Sidney will take care of that. Now, your parents."

"They've flown out of town. Dad had a conference he had to be out tomorrow for about a week. He didn't want to leave, but I told him Rylee would want him to."

Dave turned as he heard a sound from Rylee. Bending over her bed, he reached for her face, gently touching it.

"Rylee, can you hear me?"

Rylee heard Dave's voice and struggled to get past the darkness threatening her once more.

"Dave?" Her voice cracked and was barely audible.

"Right here, lass. Right here." He reached to grasp her hand. "You're safe now, sweetheart. We've got you."

Rylee nodded, then drifted off once again, her hand grasping her husband's.

Abe turned and quietly walked away. He needed some time but he also needed to talk to Frankie and Eddie.

"I'm heading downtown, Nathaniel. Call me if you need me."

Chapter 23

The man watched the Allison home, but didn't find who he was looking for. It was deserted, he thought. Now, where are they? Getting the girl would get to Dave, who would find the information he wanted from Rylee. That was how it was to work. He turned and walked away, deep in thought as to how he could find what he needed.

Michael watched him walk away, then turned a speculative eye towards Dave's home. It was dark. Good, he thought. That must mean Liana is safe. His face softened for a moment as he thought about her, then hardened again. He had a job to do and thinking about someone he once cared deeply about wouldn't help. His steps traced the path of the man's, following him to where he lived.

*****

Dave turned as the room door opened, and Liana appeared. He rose and went to hug his sister, drawing her into the room.

"Liana, you're not supposed to be here."

She nodded. "I know. Gideon's waiting to take me out to Abe's to stay. I wanted to see you two before I went." She walked towards the bed, watching as Rylee moved restlessly.

"How is she, Dave?" When he didn't respond, she turned. His eyes were on her, not his wife. "Dave?"

Dave shook his head to clear it. "Sorry, Liana. It's just I wish you hadn't come as much as you needed and wanted to." He walked over to stand by Rylee, reaching to touch her face. "She's coming back from wherever she's been. Dr. Black is still watching her heart, not saying much though."

Liana laid her hand on Dave's arm. "I'll go, Dave. I just had to see you two." Tears clogged her throat.

Dave turned and pulled his sister into a hug. "I know you did, sis. I know you did. Listen, if you need to call me, can you use someone else's phone? They know where I am, but I don't want anyone to find out where you are. Mom and Dad are safe where they are."

Liana nodded and stepped back, her eyes tracing her brother's face and then turned to her sister-in-law. "Call me if there's any change, please?" She turned and walked for the door before he could answer.

Rylee's eyes fluttered open, and she frowned, blinking to clear them. She searched the room, not sure where she was. Her eyes lighting on Dave, she tried to speak, but her throat was too dry.

Dave turned as he heard a sound, then reached to touch her face, grasping her hand.

"Rylee, you're awake. This is good. They didn't expect it for another day." As she moved restlessly, he pressed a kiss to her forehead. "You're safe, lass. You're safe."

Rylee's eyes closed and she drifted away again, her hand tucked close in Dave's. But she couldn't figure out what Dave meant or even where she was.

*****

Eddie turned as Frankie sat down beside him. "Where are we, Frankie?"

Frankie shook his head. "The men we have in custody aren't talking. Thankfully, we've been able to get their bail set really high, and they can't make it." He sighed. "But we don't have the ones who kidnapped Rylee or the one in charge." He looked up as Michael appeared in the doorway. "Now, what does he want?"

"He's been in on the investigation all along, Frankie, he just couldn't say anything. He works with the same group Rylee's Dad did." Frankie stared as Eddie rose to go meet Michael, remembering what Michael had said but not sure he even believed it.

Michael didn't sit, but stared for a moment at the two men. "What I'm about to tell you will blow my cover, but it needs to be done. The leader for them is from this town. No one would ever have suspected him. I certainly didn't." He handed over a slip of paper. "My life won't be worth much when this comes out. Just make sure you keep everyone safe." He turned and walked away, leaving the two men staring after him.

"What did he just say?" Frankie turned to Eddie, finding him staring at the paper, face whitening as he did so. "Eddie?"

Eddie handed him the paper. "We need to get Caleb back here. We won't be getting any sleep for a while, Frankie."

Frankie stared at him, then down at the paper. "Is this for real?"

Eddie nodded. "We've always suspected something like this. Michael has provided the proof we need." Eddie turned back to his chair. "Sit. We need to make plans."

*****

Caleb walked through the department heading for the conference room. Eddie met him part way through. A quick conference and Eddie headed for the outside, Caleb to the conference room.

"Where do we stand, Frankie?"

Frankie turned to face Caleb. "Did you see this coming?"

Caleb nodded. "I did. We've suspected them for years, just never had any proof to back our suspicions. Any idea where Michael is now?"

Frankie shook his head. "No. He dropped his bombshell and then walked away."

"Find him. We need to put him into protective custody. At the moment, he's the only one who can tie it all together. Who's not busy right now?"

Frankie searched the room. "Jake isn't as tied into the investigation as we are, nor is Sue. I would suggest those two."

Caleb nodded. "I'll be in my office when you need me. I'll be having to do some heavy PR work on this one, Frankie. It's not going to go the way we hope, I don't think."

Frankie watched Caleb walk away, then turned to find Jake and Sue, sending them on their way. He prayed they found Michael safe.

Caleb turned from his desk as Jake appeared in his doorway, knowing it wouldn't be good news.

"We've found Michael. Someone got to him, but he's still alive. Sue's heading in with him."

Caleb rose and walked with Jake to the conference room. "Where do we stand from that?"

"Our team's going over his room, but it was tossed. They must have thought he had some evidence hidden there." Jake stopped, a thoughtful look on his face. "They're getting desperate, Caleb. They know their time here is limited and they're trying to find the evidence first."

"That's my take on it." He turned as he heard a sound from the front of the department and groaned. "Go ahead, Jake. Get out of here. Do what you need to do to find the evidence. I'll deal with the reporters. No, they can wait. Our PR team will do that." Caleb headed into the conference room, knowing that he wouldn't be seen there.

Chapter 24

Michael turned as Dave approached him in the waiting room. The nurses and Dr. Black were with Rylee, and he had been asked to leave for a few minutes.

"Michael, I'm surprised to see you here. I heard what happened to you."

Michael gave an abrupt nod. "I don't want to be here, Dave, but I need to stay close to you two. Whether she realizes it or not, Rylee still has something they want. Donovan told me it was a game or something like that. I talked to him this morning."

"And you have been trying to stay out of sight, haven't you?"

Michael shot Dave a quick surprised look, then nodded. He had been. He didn't want to end up in protective custody and he knew that was the only option Caleb would let him have. He needed to stay on the streets to track the people responsible. Caleb's people didn't seem to be getting too far, and he knew it was only a matter of time before the men tried for Rylee again. He had slipped away from the Emergency department and made his way to Rylee's floor.

"I have. So far, I've managed to elude the detectives Frankie's sent after me. It's only a matter of time, though, until they do find me again." He looked past Dave to the room door. "How's your wife?"

"Improving but slowly. Dr. Black is still concerned about her heart. It's not responding as quickly as he hoped."

"Her heart?"

Dave nodded. "There seems to have been some damage done from the hypothermia." Dave stopped, needing to compose himself. "I just wish I could help find those monsters." He stared into the distance, jaw clenching as he struggled with his emotions. He turned tortured eyes to Michael. "Why, Michael? What is so important in what she may know?"

Michael stared at Dave, then looked past him once more, coming to a decision. "Rylee's father had information on not just treasures theft but also about human smuggling. It was becoming more commonplace coming into the country, both here and in Ireland. He settled here at the request of the president of our organization, to try and determine who was the leader. We think he had found out, and that's why he was killed. But he didn't get the information to us. Rylee seems to still have it in her possession."

"And until you get it, she'll be in danger." Dave turned to pace, Joseph keeping an eye on him. He spun, returning to Michael. "What actually are you looking for? He wouldn't have written it down."

Michael shook his head. "No, we know he didn't. We're just not sure how he saved it. Someone suggested a flash drive, but he wasn't into computers."

"So that means it could be in any form." Dave paced again. "Listen, Michael, I don't like to leave Rylee, but let's head to my place. I can go through what she brought with her. Maybe it's there somewhere."

Michael nodded. "That's sounds good. Did she bring something that looked like a game?"

Dave shrugged. "I'm not really sure. She set things away in cupboards until we could sort through what we wanted to put out. There's not a lot, I know. Just let me tell Joseph where we're heading."

Dave headed towards Joseph, then stopped as Dr. Black stepped from the room.

"Dave, just who I wanted to see. Good news. Rylee's heart is settling back into normalcy. She's rousing more and more, so by tomorrow I suspect I can move her to a regular room."

"That's good news. The nurses will be with her for a while?"

Dr. Black nodded. "They will. They have some more treatments to give her." He stopped to assess Dave. "You need to go home and get cleaned up, young man. You don't want to scare your wife."

Dave gave a half-hearted laugh. "That's what I was hoping to do." He watched as the physician walked away, then turned to Joseph. "Who else is here with you?"

Joseph narrowed his eyes. What was Dave asking? "Luke and Micah are here.

Luke is just down the hall, Micah on the main floor. Matt is headed our way as well."

"I'm heading back to my place. Have Matt meet me there. Michael's coming with me. I'll pick up Micah on the way out." He turned in a circle. "I don't like the feeling I'm getting, Joseph. Can Luke stay in the room with Rylee until I'm back?"

"That's not a problem. I see Jake and Sue are here as well."

Dave turned. "Keep them here with you, please?" Dave disappeared towards Michael, pulling him with him to the elevators, grabbing the first available one.

Jake turned and stared towards the elevators. Why did he feel that Michael had been here?

"Where's Dave?" Sue stared at Joseph, trying to read his face.

"Dr. Black sent him home to get cleaned up. I guess he figured Dave's present appearance would scare Rylee."

Jake and Sue exchanged glances, frustrated that Dave had left. They both felt he knew where Michael was.

"Have you seen Michael?" Jake watched Joseph's face closely.

"Michael? Who's he?" Joseph didn't let on that he knew full well who Michael was, but he wanted to give the two men time to get away.

*****

Dave pulled out the last box Rylee had stashed in a cupboard. Is it here, Lord? Can we really end this by finding whatever it is her father gave her? He opened the box, sorting through what was there. His hands froze as he stared at the small box in front of him. He slowly took hold of it, raising it from the box, and setting it on the table. His eyes met Michael. How much could he really trust him? Liana seemed to think he could fully trust him, but he hadn't seen Michael in many years.

"What do you have, Dave?" Michael's quiet question crossed the silence between the two men, Micah and Matt looking on.

"I'm not sure, Michael. This box matches the one Rylee found earlier." He carefully opened it to reveal smooth oval stones. "What are these?" Dave tipped them out, rolling one around in his hand. "Wait, there's etching on it. What is this?"

Michael reached for it, holding it to get a good look at it. "This is it, Dave. This is what they're looking for." He looked around, an anxious look on his face. "We need to get these to Frankie and Eddie. They can work with these now. What he had in the other box goes with these."

Michael rose and paced, thoughts racing through his mind. How to get them there?

Matt stepped away to take a call, returning with a grim look on his face.

"Joseph just called. Jake and Sue just arrested two men trying to get to Rylee. From what he overheard, they're her kidnappers." He pointed at Dave and then Michael. "We need to get you two out of here now."

Dave spun at the harsh tone in Matt's voice, then nodded. He scooped the stones back into the box and handed it to him.

"Here, you take these. They won't expect any other than Michael or me to have them. Take us back to the hospital, then head for Frankie or Eddie.”

*****

Dave sank back into his chair beside Rylee, Michael settling down on the couch near the window. Joseph had insisted the two men stay together. Micah paced the room near the door, knowing Luke and Joseph were outside. All of the men knew it had come to a crisis and would do their utmost to keep Dave, Rylee, and Michael safe.

Joseph looked up as the elevator opened and Abe walked towards him, stern lines on his face. Caleb was beside him, matching him step for step.

“Joseph, they’re safe?” Abe’s question reached Joseph before he did.

Joseph nodded. “We put them all together. Caleb, did Matt make it to you?”

Caleb looked around before he spoke. “Matt did. His parcel is now in the hands of Eddie and Frankie. They’re working through what we have. Sue and Jake were heading over to get the arrest and search warrants.” He sighed. “I just wish Michael had come forward before now. Maybe we could have avoided all this.”

“Murphy would tell you God had a plan and purpose for this, Caleb.” Joseph gave him a cheeky grin, then sobered. “I agree with you, and I’m sure Dave does too.”

Abe stared at the door for a moment before turning to Joseph. “How’s Rylee?”

“Dave said good news. The cardiologist is pleased with her progress.” He looked past Abe. “We have company. And I don’t think you’re going to be happy, Caleb.”

Caleb turned, facing the couple walking towards him. *Why now, Lord? What are they doing here? They have absolutely no reason to be on this floor or to be near Dave and Rylee or even Michael.*

“Chief, we’ve come to see how Rylee Allison is.” The man held out his hand to Caleb, then dropped it with a frown when Caleb didn’t respond. “Did you hear me, Chief?”

“I did, but no one goes into that room. She’s under protective custody.”

"That doesn't mean us, young man." The elegantly dressed woman moved to brush past him, and both Joseph and Abe stepped into her way. "What is the meaning of this? Tell those men to move."

"I can't do that. They don't work for me. They're hired by someone private. I don't give them orders."

"But you do. You're the police chief, at least for now, you are." The man's pompous attitude rubbed the three men wrong.

"Sorry, but that's how it is." Caleb caught sight of Jake and Sue heading his way and sighed a breath of relief. Jake had held up paperwork for him to see. "We'll move this downtown to finish our discussion."

"I don't think so." The woman once more moved to go past the men, but stopped as a hand touched her arm. "Get your hands off me." She spun to face Sue. "What are you doing?"

Sue glanced at Caleb and at his nod, reached for her handcuffs. "You're under arrest, Mrs. Stone."

"Arrest? On what charges?"

Caleb nodded as Jake read Elias Stone his rights, despite his protests.

"Smuggling.   Theft.   Kidnapping. Attempted murder. Assault. Conspiracy to all of these. We're still sorting through all the charges." Caleb nodded to Jake and Sue. "Take them back to headquarters, separately please. They'll want their lawyers, but we'll be holding off on that for a bit, until we speak with the prosecutor." He looked at the couple, a banker and his wife, and shook his head. "I don't get it. I don't suppose I ever well."

The three men watched as the couple were led away, uniformed officers there to walk the detectives and their suspects out.

"Is that it now, Caleb? Are Rylee and Dave safe?" Abe's voice finally broke the silence.

"I pray they are. Eddie said they had everyone in custody except that couple."

Joseph spoke. "No one would ever have suspected them, now would they?"

Caleb turned to look at him. "No, no one ever would. Now, let's go see Dave and

Michael and let them know what's gone down."

Three months later, Rylee turned as she felt Dave running his hand down her braid. She expected to be handed the hair tie, but Dave's hand just rested on her back. She tilted her head to watch him, taking in the contented look on his face.

"Dave?"

He turned to look down at Rylee, amazed that he had found such a woman to love. No, he thought, God brought her into my life and through her example to heal me.

"Rylee, I'm just so thankful for you." He dropped a kiss on her mouth, then wrapped her in his arms, his eyes going to the back of the house where their families had gathered. "We've been through a time, but God has brought healing in so many different ways."

Rylee continued to study the man she loved. "He has, love, that He has. People think that when the woman touched Christ's garment, she only had physical healing, but I have always thought she had much more healing that that. God heals us in ways we can't imagine or expect, although sometimes He doesn't." She stopped, her thoughts confused for a moment.

"I know what you're meaning, lass." Dave's chin rested on the top of her head. She was just the right height for him to do that. "Our healing is dependent on Him. All we can do is ask and trust." He looked past his parents talking with Ailynne to where his sister and Michael stood.

"You're watching Liana, aren't you?" Not much missed Rylee.

"I am. They make a cute couple, you know. I never thought they would. I knew there was interest there, but then Michael left so quickly."

Rylee nodded. "I asked him about that one day. He said God had told him to go, do what He was asking him to do and to trust. Michael obeyed in a way that left many wondering, but he knew that he had to. Did you know he had spoken to Liana before he left?"

Dave shook his head. "No, I didn't, but now that you mention it, it doesn't surprise me. By the looks of it, we'll be gaining a brother-in-law in the near future."

"We will. Your parents are happy. Gran is content now that she can cut back hours at the shop, with Liana wanting to learn Gran's secrets. Donovan and Fergus are settled, each with their own sweetheart now." Rylee leaned back on Dave, feeling his strength behind her. "Despite what we went through, Dave, I never stopped trusting God."

"I know what you mean, Rylee." He paused, then continued, "Ken is still after me to take on a supervisor position."

"And your answer?"

"That I will pray about it, discuss it with you and then let him know. He just asked that it not be ten years from now."

Rylee laughed at the thought. "Somehow I don't think it will. You've made up your mind, haven't you, my love? You'll do well in that position."

Dave tilted his head to stare at her. "How did you know?"

She shrugged. "I just did. I'm coming to know the man I married."

Dave and Rylee stood and watched their families, content in their world. They knew there would be difficulties, illnesses, death but they also knew the Great Physician and trusted fully in His care.

Dear Readers

Thank you for choosing to read the story of Dave and Rylee. This story, based on the verses of the woman with the issue who reached out in faith to touch Christ's garment, has been a story I have wanted to write for years. It's been there in my mind, but I just didn't have the characters to do so. That is, until Dave started appearing in previous novels. Rylee, a lovely Irish lady, brings in the heritage I have, that of northern Ireland.

How does God heal? Who does He heal? That is something we can't answer. Our duty is to ask and trust. Christ is our Great Physician, and we have all been recipients at some point of healing. When I look at the story of the woman in the Bible, I see not just physical healing, but her heart and emotions were healed as well. She had faith enough to reach out. God can heal each aspect of our body, minds and souls. We just need to reach out and ask for that touch, to reach out ourselves in faith, knowing He hears.

A big thank you to friend and fellow author, Jean West, for taking time from her busy life and proofreading this novel for me.

God bless each one of you who have read this novel. My prayer, as always, is that it will have challenged you to reach deeper into your walk with God.

Ronna